The Black Manor

Sue Carpenter

Sue Carpenter

Contents

Prologue

The man walked through the raging storm to take shelter in the rustic shed, thunder clapped outside, and he wiped water off his face as he slammed the door. The three men inside turned their attention to their boss. 'He's found out,' he boomed.

'Wait, what'll we do?' his lanky friend replied from inside the shed while patting a bright yellow and red parrot on his shoulder.

'Kill him,' the boss shrugged like it was no big deal.

'Ha, ha! Sure, you will,' Lanky snorted, stuffing a maggot through some bars to feed the caged kiwi. The other two snickered until the sound was cut short by the big man's growl.

'We all will, I have a plan.'

The laughter died away as the plotting started.

Chapter 1: The Sad News
Belinda

'Class dismissed,' the teacher called.

I grinned and glanced over at Brandon, my boyfriend,

'No maths today.' Brandon squeezed my hand.

'Come over,' I stood up from my desk, sliding my hand into my boyfriend Brandon's, we could finally have some time together.

'Practice,' his friend said, pulling him away from me.

'Sorry.' He gave me a quick kiss before running off, chanting like a jock. I used to come before hockey, homework, and everything.

'Wait.' I said so quietly that no one hears. I don't even know what to say. Wait, spend time with me instead? Wait, if you want to choose them over me, we are done?

Wait, pick me instead? Wait, or at least turn around and look at me? He didn't. I had a book to read instead. One without hockey in it – about becoming a vet in New Zealand.

My ponytail swayed side to side as I stomped home through the alleyway. Crossing the road, I headed towards my place down the long driveway with roses on one side and trees on the other. The trees produced seeds that in the rain, when you drove over them, or crushed them some other way, they turned into natural stink bombs. Thankfully, it wasn't raining today so no sour smell. But regardless, stink was how I was feeling.

I was over Brandon fobbing me off. A few months ago, I used to sneak Brandon home with me on days like those. Lately, he hadn't been so keen. I kicked at a loose stone on the driveway, hurtling it into the fence. Today, it was his loss. It was my loss! Why didn't he want to be with me?

I paused at the sight of our old yellow Mazda in the driveway. What was Mum doing home early? Maybe the power was out at her work, which happened once before, but as I reached the back door, Mum appeared, and her face told another story. Her makeup had washed down her face and the twinkle had died in her eyes.

Normally Mum had a beautiful face, round and pale, with caring blue eyes that always made me feel loved, even when I disappointed her. Thankfully, I looked a lot like Mum, as I didn't want to look like my loser of a dad at all.

'Come here Belinda, I've got some news,' Mum said, opening her arms out for me.

Uh-oh. Mum used my full name, not the shortened Bee that I insisted on. Something was really wrong. I braced myself as Mum ran her hand through her short, spiky hair, making it stick up more than usual, emphasizing how distressed she looked.

'What did Dad do this time?' I asked.

'I wish! Your Dad I can handle. Come here.' Mum squeezed me tight as she took a deep breath. 'Uncle Jerry has died.'

My chest constricted. I turned to Mum, disbelieving. 'What?'

Mum squeezed me tighter. 'I'm sorry, honey. I know the two of you were close. We're all going to miss him.'

'But … he was so healthy and active. We only saw him a few months ago. He had more energy than Uncle Charlie, even though he's, like, three times as old. How could he have died so suddenly?'

Mum lifted her hand to smooth a wayward strand of my hair. Normally, I'd shrug away from her when she did that. I was getting too old to be fussed over. But right now, it was comforting.

'People Uncle Jerry's age die. He's had a great innings. We should be thankful he led such a great life. He had all his animals to keep him busy, and he had us to come visit. Some people aren't so lucky.'

She turned and absently started clearing dishes, putting away the cereal boxes we'd hurriedly abandoned that morning in our rush to leave for work and school. 'We have to pack. Your aunt and uncle will be here soon. We're all travelling together for the funeral.' Funeral. It was really real then. I looked over at the corner where a birdcage hung from a stand. Inside, my parrot, Marmalade, eyed me sadly. Like she knew my heart was breaking. She let out a squawk and chirruped, 'The keys in the flowerpot!'

Tears filled my eyes, and I tried to hold them back, but they rolled down my face, anyway. Mum was right, of course. Uncle Jerry had a good life. But he'd stepped in and become my second grandfather, after his brother, my real grandfather, had passed at a young age. And he'd been the best surrogate grandfather ever. Was it selfish to want him for longer?

'We've got about an hour before my sister will be here to pick us up.'

'It's weird that we're going in the same car,' I said. Never, done that before.

'She is trying to make a point to Charlie about why they needed the seven-seater.'

A giggle escaped. I loved Uncle Charlie, and he loved to be right. I would go to the ends of the earth to prove him wrong, as would his wife and daughters.

The first thing I packed was Marmalade. She was easy to pack as she had a clear bag and food ready all the time for adventures. Marmalade was my feathered dog. Some people took their dogs everywhere, while I took my bird.

'You can't bring Marmalade,' Mum said when I got to the lounge with my bags.

'No way I'm leaving her, Mum. Uncle Jerry gave me Marmalade. He would be so hurt if we didn't bring her.' At the very thought, I started to cry. I was crying about losing Uncle Jerry, not leaving Marmalade, but I couldn't handle any other bad news.

Technically speaking, Uncle Jerry had also given us our cats, rabbits and fish, and I wasn't fighting to bring them too. Even I knew there were limits, and I had already arranged for the neighbour to feed them. But Marmalade was different. Without her, I knew I couldn't face the loss of Uncle Jerry.

A beep stopped any further discussion as a gold seven-seater drove into our driveway. I grabbed my gear, including my bird, and went and sat in the back seat with Cindy. As soon as we got in the car, the chatter started.

'I can't believe he's no longer with us,' I said to Cindy, my first cousin and best friend.

Cindy, like her dad, was a redhead with freckles, and she was the cutest of us all.

Everyone muttered words along the same lines as mine.

'Remember that time you made him that hat out of drinking straws, Bee?' Charlie said. 'And he wore it all day!' Uncle Charlie didn't like to be called uncle because he said it made him sound old. Which, of course, made me want to call him Uncle Charlie even more!

'And the next two visits,' Lily held up two fingers. Lily and Sofie, the twins a year older than Cindy and I, sat in the middle seats together.

'I loved the berries he bought at Christmas,' Sofie added laughing. 'I missed them last year.' The twins were identical and looked like their Mum, my Mum and me, although they made a lot of effort not to look like each other. Lily always had her hair coloured lighter and shorter, Sofie's sense of humor was darker like her hair.

'What will happen to his stuff?' Cindy asked.

'All his pets?' I added, thinking of Basil, his beautiful black and white spotted dog that followed him and me everywhere.

'I hoped we could take Basil, if that's okay with you?' Mum asked her sister. My heart softened; I loved my Mum – she understood.

'Gee, don't you have enough pets?' Charlie laughed.

'More than happy with that,' Aunty Carol replied.

'We sure don't want a dog.' Uncle Charlie rubbed his temples. 'Well, whoever inherits will have a lot of decisions to make. I only hope Uncle Jerry doesn't have a lot of debts. Otherwise, the entire estate will have to be sold off. I dare say we might have to pay for his funeral if he hasn't made provision for it himself. Does he even own his house?'

'He owns it, I think,' I said. 'He once told me that his house is very special. Full of family memories.'

'Well, that may have to be sold, too. I guess we'll be busy sorting everything out over the next few days. You girls might have to entertain yourselves for a while if that happens,' Charlie said. 'We want to avoid the same nightmare I had with my parents' estate.'

'He may have left everything to SPCA,' Cindy said. 'He loved animals, and my friend's gran did that. Her family was gutted.'

'Let's not worry about any of that. We should make it north in time. The funeral home will try to stay open for us so we can see Jerry tonight if we want.'

'Ouch,' I rubbed my arm where Cindy punched me at the yellow car heading our way. Lily rubbed her arm too. We always play the yellow car punching game when we travel and today it was a great distraction.

We listened to Queen the rest of the way north, singing off pitch and laughing. We normally laughed more and today's cheer felt put-on, but made the trip easier. Lily and I got the others the next time we saw a double yellow.

'I have missed you,' I whispered to Cindy. We were squeezed in the back seats, our bags and Marmalade on our laps.

'You too, I have so much to tell you – when we are alone.'

'I guess there's a guy by the look of your skimpy outfit and painted face,' I teased Cindy.

'My clothes are no skimpier than theirs,' she said, pointing to the twins.

'That's debatable.' I laughed, thinking she was wrong. The twins spent a lot of time on their appearance – but mainly so that they didn't look alike. They were in jeans. Cindy's skirt looked like a belt!

We made it to the funeral home just after four-thirty in the afternoon.

'Do you guys want to come say goodbye?'

'What! To his corpse?' Sofie asked. 'Don't think so.'

'Solid pass.' I wanted to remember his loving and kind face, his twinkling eyes and chubby cheeks, not a pale version. A shiver ran up my spine just thinking about his body alone in a box. As we girls sat out in the front waiting, four guys arrived.

'OMG, look how cute that guy is.' Cindy giggled.

'Who? The one covered in tats?' I laughed.

'The young blonde.'

He looked to be in his twenties, well built, with blonde hair waving off his face. He stood out as the others looked like an eclectic mix of scariness. One of them was covered in tattoos. They looked like they'd tried to dress up nice but missed the mark. Although we were only sixteen, the blond couldn't take his eyes off Cindy. Mind you, with the short skirt Cindy was wearing, all the men glanced at her long legs.

One of them said, 'Jerry had no family. I wonder what he wanted done with his body.'

'Are you talking about Jerry Loveridge?' I said as I stood up. They all turned to me.

'Yip,' said a guy who looked to be in his thirties and had a scar on his cheek.

'Why do you think he had no family?' I asked.

'He had no children or wife,' an older looking, well-built man replied.

That man smelt like he hadn't had a shower in a week and had overcompensated by spraying deodorant all over himself. The overpowering BO and musky smell made me want to gag. I walked towards the men as my cousins stood. Mum, Cindy's parents and a man headed our way. I reached out to shake the men's hands and introduced myself. 'I am Belinda Loveridge. Nice to meet you. Jerry was close to his brother, and we most definitely considered him family. How did you know my Uncle Jerry?'

They all looked shocked, like I had stabbed them in the back.

Mum headed over, looking alarmed. I turned to introduce her to the men, not that I knew who they were.

'I think these guys are friends of Uncle Jerry's,' I said to Mum before turning back to them to confirm. 'Is that right?'

The youngest one reached out to shake my hand and said, 'I'm Damion Curtain, and I worked for your Uncle Jerry. We all did. We all live in his place and are uncertain what's happening with our jobs and accommodation now. Murray over here,' he said, pointing to the man with the tatts, 'is the one who found Jerry this morning and called the police.'

The funeral director spoke at this point. 'You found him this morning? When did any of you last see him?'

The men all looked at each other and after an awkward silence Murray said, 'Maybe Saturday, or Friday, not sure. The days all roll into each other because we've been busy.'

Uncle Charlie addressed the entire group, 'we have just made plans for the funeral;

it will be the day after tomorrow. Hope you can all make it. We'll meet the lawyers and accountant tomorrow and sort out his business. I didn't realise he had so many staff members. He always told us he ran a small pet shop.'

The men laughed. 'It's not a small pet shop.'

The youngest man was still laughing but now faced Cindy. 'We're glad he had a funeral plan; Jerry had this side of things all sorted and paid for. That's one less thing to worry about.'

'We can meet you at the accountants. We were all business partners with him,' Murray said with authority.

'Do you mind if we follow you back to the house? We've always met Jerry in town when we have visited.' Mum said.

'Sorry, we're just gonna go down to the pub to have a drink, in Jerry's honour, you know,' said a tall, lanky man.

'That sounds like a brilliant plan,' said Charlie, grinning and rubbing his hands together till he saw his wife's face. 'Oh, next time, maybe,' he muttered.

'Yeah, mate. Maybe next time,' said Damion, though he didn't sound enthused. He glanced at the others and jerked his head toward the door. 'We better get going.'

Murray, who looked like he was the one in charge, subtly shook his head at the others.

We headed towards our car. I opened the door and got Marmalade and his bag out, and I started talking to Marmalade.

The tall lanky man ran over to me and said, 'Is that Marmalade?'

I looked at him, surprised. 'You know my bird?'

He was extremely excited to see Marmalade. Grinning and jiggling about from foot to foot. He just kept looking at my bird, making me feel uncomfortable. Why was he hanging about? What a weirdo! I wished he'd just go away.

Finally, he said, 'Marmalade, you haven't changed at all!' Then he looked at me. 'I raised her from an egg, and she was so easy to train. Who's a good girl?' he said to Marmalade.

'Good girl,' Marmalade squawked back.

That guy may be odd, but he sure loved my bird. Maybe we could get along after all.

'We gotta go, Nigel,' Murray called from a twin cab ute with '*The Biggest Little Pet Shop*' written on its door.

I let out a breath as they drove off, glad to see them go, and not just because the air was fresher after they'd gone. Something about them wasn't right. 'Those guys were weird,' I said.

'Not the cute one,' Cindy whispered.

The twins laughed.

'Stop looking for a scandal everywhere, Bee.' Sofie chuckled.

'They found a dead body. Of course, they'll be weird. Wouldn't you?' Lily said.

'I guess,' I lied. That wasn't fear – I trusted most people – just not that Murray guy! He was hiding something, and I was determined to find out what. Thankfully, within the paperwork the lawyer, Mr Wade, had left for us at the funeral home, there were keys and a map to Uncle Jerry's house, so we followed the directions.

Chapter 2: Manor bound
Belinda

On the drive to Uncle Jerry's, we stopped at a set of lights in the middle of town, where I gazed at the shimmering ocean. Beside the car a group of locals throwing a rugby ball ran along the riverbank, roughly charging at each other. If only I could join them and be carefree for fifteen minutes. Uncle Charlie let one rip.

'Oh, Dad!'

'Gross.' His daughters squealed.

The boy charging with the rugby ball must have heard the commotion in the van as he turned to look at us. Our eyes held until he was tackled. We had driven off before I saw him emerge. My cheeks expanded as I held in a laugh. The township disappeared into farmlets, then larger farms.

'Jerry didn't live on a farm, did he?' Aunty Carol said. No one replied. None of us knew.

How sad was that? Why had we not insisted on visiting his place? We all became silent; I could almost hear the gravel under the tyres. I wanted to plead for Mum to put the music back on, but I would not be the one to break the silence. I got lost in watching the farms we passed. Until we slowed and the car indicator clicked over the silence.

'This is gorgeous,' I said being the first to talk after all. We turned down a driveway lined with fruit trees. More fruit-laden trees blocked the view of the front of the house. It opened onto an expansive parking area, revealing a magnificent house that looked like a large black castle.

Sofie said, 'Oh, it's a black manor.'

That described it perfectly. The Black Manor. A gigantic mansion all painted in matt black with ivy growing up the walls. 'Oh, it's beautiful,' I sighed, lifting my phone to take a photo. I wanted to remember this moment, this place. A warming sensation in my chest definitely told me that there was something special here.

'This house has room for Uncle Jerry and the four men that we saw at the funeral home, and the pets and animals that he bred for his pet shop, and all of us,' I said, surprised at the size of the house, I mean castle. It took ages for Uncle Charlie to drive around the back and park the car in the carport. There were lots of corrugated buildings that backed on to the wide driveway. Was one of them a garage?

After hopping out of the car, we all paused quietly. I could hear sheep in the distance, but louder than that we could hear birds. Lots of birds. Even louder was Marmalade screeching out in a noise I had never heard from her. 'Home?' I asked her.

'Home,' she replied as I carried her carrier to the large wooden veranda.

'And the local zoo...' Charlie joked.

We opened the front door and wandered into the house. There were no photos on the walls, nothing that would reveal anything about our family to strangers, but at the same time, to us, it was all about our family. Any tears I had held on to when we arrived at the farm escaped.

'Look at the drinking straw hat,' Cindy laughed, wiping her own eyes. She pointed to the objects displayed inside a cabinet. The art on the walls were paintings that we had given Uncle Jerry as Christmas presents. Mum picked up a blanket draped over the back of the large green chair by the fireplace. It was one I'd sent Uncle Jerry after he'd given me a knitting kit one year for Christmas. The candles on the fireplace mantel were ones we had made at school as fundraising for a school camp to Camp Te ao mārama a few years back.

'My tie-died cushions,' Lily, pointed at the cushion she'd made for him. I imagine to anyone else looking at this lounge, it didn't look like Uncle Jerry had a family. But for the seven of us standing at the door, we could see just how much we'd all meant to him. So much of our life was here in this room. We found the kitchen and sat down, and Mum made us all hot chocolates before we headed off to find bedrooms for the night. The twins shared a room, as did Cindy and me. We took the four closest rooms to the dining area, so we were all near to each other. Everyone went off to bed half an hour later. It had been a long day, and we were all exhausted.

Cindy and I snuggled into our beds, but then I sat up. 'Crap, I just remembered I have a speech due. It was worth five percent of my end-of-year exam. Do you think my teacher will let me email it to him? I'll have to find out in the morning.'

'You nerd.' She laughed before rolling over. It wasn't even five minutes before her breathing slowed.

As everyone else slept, I lay awake. A strange scratching sound, low and grating, rumbled from somewhere downstairs. Then there was a whine. Was it some kind of animal in pain? I sat up to listen and heard it again. Longer this time. It cut off with a sharp yelp, raising bumps all over my skin. I got up to investigate. First, I thought the noise was coming from the kitchen, but the only noise in there was the hum of the refrigerator. I went into the lounge and stopped to listen. There it was again, coming from outside. It must have been one of the animals. I opened the front door and called, 'Basil.'

The minute I called his name, he appeared. My favourite little black and white Jack Russell. 'My good boy. It is good to see you again.' I patted him as he panted.

My Uncle Jerry was close to his dog. They were best friends. 'Where have you been?'

I picked him up, and he was light. Lost weight. His collar that I'd made him was missing. I walked to the kitchen and gave him water, which he drank while I looked for dog food. I couldn't find any but found some left over sausages and he enjoyed them.

Sitting on Uncle Jerry's chair, I patted Basil until his breathing relaxed, then I put him on the dog bed and covered him with a pet blanket. When I left him in his bed, he followed me down the hall. 'Are you missing Jerry? Come on, then.' We entered my room and snuggled together to comfort each other until we fell asleep.

A few hours later, a car pulled up outside, waking me. I guessed it was the guys coming back from the pub. I got up, intending to tell them what rooms we were sleeping in. They had all been dusty, so we assumed we were not in their rooms – but imagine the fright if they walked in not expecting to see us.

As I made my way down the hall lit by moonlight, the security light flicked on outside the lounge. Before I got the chance to say anything, I heard them talking.

'Jerry's family is gonna be a bit of a problem. What will we do if they start sniffing around the animals?' It sounded like Damion.

'Nothing,' Nigel said. 'They will be here for a day, then they'll go, and that'll be the end of it.'

Shocked at what they were saying, I slumped on the chair, Basil followed, then curled up and fell asleep again.

What about the business? What if he leaves the business to them?' Damion said.

'He won't. He always said the business was all of ours, so we will be fine. If not, we all have enough money put away to buy them out. Don't worry, they have no idea what this operation is worth. We can put in a low offer. They'll be grateful to have the whole thing off their hands.' Murray told them.

'I'm for that.' The tall, gangly one's shadow nodded in agreement outside the sheer curtain. 'Even if we have to get a mortgage, with the way the business is going, we will have paid it off in a year, easy.'

Damion, Cindy's eye candy, said, 'Well, I'm off to check on the little beasts now. The rest of you off to bed.'

'We'll have a shuffle of the animals and birds in case anyone comes around snooping early in the morning, so get some sleep for now.'

Then three of the men crowded into the lounge.

On Uncle Jerry's lazy boy chair, I pretended to be asleep. When they turned the light on, they saw me and took a step back. I acted as if I had just been woken up. Rubbing my eyes, I patted Basil.

I said, 'Hi, I hope you had fun at the pub. Hope we are not in your rooms; the others are all settled in for the night. Mr Wade left a key for us, which was good because we lost you at the funeral home. You took off before we could ask where we should sleep.' I took a breath after rambling. The men looked at each other like possums staring into a car's headlights and I lifted the blanket from my knees and said, 'I made this blanket for Uncle Jerry; he was very special to me.

Anyway, I better get to bed. Do you mind if I take Basil with me? He was sad. I'm not sure where he normally sleeps, but Basil has always stayed with me when they visited us. Basil and I have a special connection, too. See you in the morning.' I took another breath in the now silent room. Only the grandfather clock ticked. 'Mum bought a lot of bacon, eggs, and sausages. We will have a big brekkie cook up to get to know you guys. See you then. Good night.' I left the room, and the men had still not spoken.

I could tell they had no idea we were going to be there, which is why they'd spoken so openly. My suspicions about them had been right. They were anxious that we kept away from the animals. I would find out why.

Chapter 3: Mine

Belinda

The next day we had the big breakfast cook-up, but none of the four men showed up, even though that morning Mum and Aunty told us they had also invited them.

The lawyer, Mr Wade, arrived after nine. He said he was prepared to read the will, and that Jerry's will had never changed, even though he had kept in regular contact with Jerry until last week. I told Mum what I had heard the men saying last night: that the business was theirs and they had expected Uncle Jerry to leave everything to them. Mr Wade asked Mum, 'Are you Belinda Loveridge?'

'Oh, no, that's me. I stuck up my hand like I was in school. Seriously. I really was a nerd. His eyebrows rose before he spoke to Mum again. 'Are you Belinda's mum?'

'Yes, I am.' She crossed her arms, looking puzzled. ''Do you mind if Belinda and I go for a walk?' Mum and I looked at each other. This was a bit weird, but when I glanced back at the lawyer, curiosity got the better of me and I ended up shrugging. 'Sure.' Wherever I went, Basil came too, so Mr Wade, Basil and I headed out for a walk. We went through a gate and strolled along a track next to a paddock full of sheep. After a natural silence, Mr Wade spoke.

'Your Uncle Jerry spoke highly of you Belinda; I am, however, surprised you are so young.'

'I loved Uncle Jerry too. We're all going to miss him.'

'Jerry always hoped that you would love it here as much as he and your grandad did.'

Mr Wade opened his folder and handed me a black-and-white photo of two little boys running around in front of the same house we could now see in the distance.

'Uncle Jerry and Granddad,' I said instantly.

'What do you think of this place?' he asked me.

I opened my arms out wide, taking it all in and did a spin, 'Look at it, it's amazing, like a dream, the animals, the large open spaces, the trees, all of it.'

Mr Wade laughed but then his face turned serious, 'I can see why he wanted to leave this place to you.'

I jolt to a stop, 'M-m-me.' I managed to get out, 'why me?'

'He wanted you to be older, of course. Although he had started to slow down a bit, he still thought he had more gas in the tank. He wanted to bring you here and train you on the farm himself when you finished school.'

'This is too much' I gasped, so much to process. 'But what about his workers, I thought Uncle Jerry would want them to take over this place?'

'Uh.... I guess that seemed like the logical choice, but...' The lawyer scratched the back of his neck, I crossed my arms and eyed him up, what's he not telling me are all four of them dodgy or something?'

'Jerry felt something was wrong with them but couldn't put his finger on it, so I have been looking into it. Last week, I discovered that their names are all fake. I want you to know I am still working on it and hope that you will be able to replace them soon.'

I exhaled. 'So, I have a business, a house, and potential dodgy staff members, along with all the animals I don't know how to care for?'

How was I supposed to handle all that at only sixteen? Thankfully, Mum was an accountant, and she could do the books. But would Mum let us stay here?

'This is crazy.'

'You will get support. I have Mark, the vet, coming out to help you. We are going to say that Jerry had booked him in to look at the stock. Mark has not been allowed here for five years and your Uncle Jerry has been pushing for it. Those men were too controlling. Mark is on standby for when he is allowed to come here. He will help teach you about the stock, and we will look for farmhands for you.'

'He seriously wanted to leave the place just for me?' I looked at the green paddocks and trees.

'Yes, he wanted to, and he always has. He shouted us all at the pub the day you told him you were going to study to be a vet.'

'I'm still at school.'

Mr Wade handed me a piece of paper. 'Your mum will be executor of the will until you are of age.'

I looked down at the paper in my hands. The last will of Jerry Alexander Loveridge.

I, Jerry A. Loveridge, leave all my worldly possessions, the house, business, vehicles, and money to Belinda Lee Loveridge.

Mr Wade looked at the shocked expression on my face. 'Yes Belinda, as of now, according to this official paperwork, everything that Jerry Loveridge owned is yours. I would like to talk to your mum, aunty and uncle about Jerry's concerns. It appears that the staff have a lot more money than the actual business was generating. As it was, your uncle was giving them most of the profits from the business, because they were doing most of the work. They all had free accommodation, and everybody just fed themselves, but Jerry paid the staff living expenses. The accountant investigated some things and had many concerns.'

'Woowooo! Slow down.'

I sat down on a patch of damp grass. 'This is mine?' I asked, picking some grass and holding it out to him.

'Yes,' he smiled kindly.

'I need some time to process this.'

'I know – but I need you to process that Jerry had just started to investigate it when he died. He had heard some weird noises in the middle of the night and the money didn't seem to add up. Yesterday, I spoke to the coroner. He believes Jerry's been dead for a few days, so the men lied about when they found him. I want you to watch your back because I don't know if those workers can be trusted,' Mr Wade said seriously.

'I haven't even seen any of the animals yet.'

'Living here and caring for the pets is part of the men's job description, but it's up to you and your mother to decide if you want to keep it that way. If you want them to go, by law, give them notice and you will have to make them redundant or fire them. I highly suggest that before you tell them you're the new owner, you try to get as much information out of them on the business as you can because I don't think Jerry had a lot of hands-on experience at all in the last couple of years.'

'All of this?' I repeated. 'It's too much!'

'You can sell it, but he hoped you wouldn't.'

'No, I don't want to. I love it here. I feel connected to it.'

'And to the animals,' he said, looking at Basil, who was sniffing around the ground at my feet. 'I suspect Murray, the guy who's been working for your uncle for twenty years, was manipulating and bullying Jerry quite a bit towards the end.'

As he talked and we walked around the entire property, we must have taken over an hour. I didn't know what to say about the fact that it was all mine. There were sheep and cattle paddocks and fences that hid parts from the track we were on. I assumed the parts we didn't visit were neighbouring farms. Cindy and the twins were Jerry's great-nieces, just like me. How would they feel when they found out that I'd been left everything? Would they be upset? What about Mum? I wasn't ready to deal with that.

'I'm scared to tell my family; can I take some time to process this before we tell them?'

'Yes, and I will tell them about the issues with the workers.'

'Yes please,' I said, relieved. I had struggled to take in most of what he'd said. Something about being worried the men were dodgy. I signed the paperwork with Mr Wade leaning on his back in the paddock. My paddock. It was all done and dusted. This property was mine, and I was only sixteen. I owned a family business. Mr Wade headed off to talk to the adults, but I kept walking around and thinking. The Black Manor was mine. What did that make me? Lord of the Black Manor? Or at least, Lady of the Manor? It was all so weird. I wasn't ready to tell anyone about this. I wanted to reach out to my boyfriend back home, but we'd had a bit of a fight last weekend, and he hadn't reached out to me since. Not even since I was off school yesterday, which was unlike him. Have I not crossed his mind? By the time I headed back to the house, Mr Wade had left.

I walked around the Manor in a daze until I was hit by a strong smell of musk perfume and a high-pitched laugh. I followed the cackle into the kitchen where a lady in a black blazer and short skirt with a leopard print blouse sat surrounded by paperwork. She was punching numbers into her phone.

'Hi,' I said, and set about making myself a marmite sandwich.

'Hey love, don't mind us – adult stuff,' Uncle Charlie said.

I'm sixteen and a property owner – almost an adult, I thought, taking a bite.

'You don't have to do too much to prepare. I already have a handful of people who will be keen.' The musk smelling Leopard said.

'That's great.' Uncle Charlie said.

'Just sign here and I will start with the marketing.'

'Need to wait for the will reading,' Mum said.

'What's this about?' My eyebrows creased.

'Adult stuff – run along and play,' the lady said.

'You better not be a real estate agent,' I said. I walked closer and looked at her paperwork. She was! My nose crinkled at the smell of her.

'How rude,' the musky smelling creature replied.

'Leave us for a few moments please, Bee,' Mum asked, standing up.

My heart pounded; she had no right. I normally rode the wave, not this time. This place was mine. 'No' I yelled – noise actually came out, 'this place is not for sale.' Tears burned my cheeks, and I wanted to grab her papers and throw them everywhere, but I was not a child. They'd no right to sell the manor. It was mine – they just didn't know it yet.

'I have all I need; just give me a call and I will set the ball rolling,' she said, gathering her paperwork into two piles, one for her to take and one to leave. I would destroy what she left, but in a civilised way when no one was watching.

The dust from her red convertible had settled, yet I was still pacing. I couldn't tell my family yet – I needed some time to get used to it first, but what if I lost the property while I waited? Maybe I should call Mr Wade back. To calm down, I headed to see the birds. The tall lanky guy was walking into the aviary with a sack of birdseed, so I followed him.

I walked over to him and said, 'Hi, not sure if you remember, but my name is Bee. What's your name?'

He turned, a little startled, 'I'm Nigel.'

'Hi, Nigel. Uncle Jerry taught me everything I know about animals. Can you please give me a tour? I'd love to know more. I'd love to hear more about Basil and Marmalade. Does Marmalade have any family here?'

He couldn't help but talk to me all about Marmalade. If he trained my amazing bird, he must be a great guy. Nigel - the birdman. He gave me a quick tour of the small animal shed. There was a bench with containers of food stacked under it and photos of the animals and what they should eat and what they should not. How wonderful! Then I took in the animals. There were not five animals; there was more like fifty. Of each breed of each type. Inside there were mice, rats, baby hedgehogs and guinea pigs. All colours and sizes. Thankfully, they were in enormous cages and looked healthy and well cared for.

Oh, my gosh! They were all mine. All those little mouths that I was now responsible for feeding. We walked past a bigger but older shed. He pointed, 'That shed has all the dangerous chemicals that we use for pesticides, never go in there, it's not safe.' The excessive padlocks on the door stood out. The locks, unlike the rest of the shed, were not rusty – they looked brand new.

'Promise,' I said before silently adding - *promise that's the first one I will sneak into.*

Next, we went to the aviary. When I'd walked around with Mr Wade, I'd seen what I thought was an orchard. I hadn't realised that it was an aviary. It was surrounded by trees on the outside, so the aviary was camouflaged. Inside were lots of cages, lots of birds, but also more trees and bushes. In the middle of the space, it looked like a bar – only instead of alcohol there were seeds and nuts. And again, photos and charts with which breed of bird liked which foods. I turned a full circle, marveling at all the birds. They were everywhere, tweeting, pecking and fluttering. One was splashing water from a bath, it didn't smell repulsive like our town aviary did. A pair of lovebirds flew over to drink from their bowl, doves cooed, lorikeets were whistling, and cockatiels tweeted away to each other.

'These are Marmalade's brothers and those over there are also Marmalade's brothers. The two of them aren't the same breed, but we crossbred and made Marmalade, the most beautiful bird we ever created. I was devastated when I came home, and Jerry told me that Marmalade had gone. Jerry said that he had a found her a great new home. Didn't know where until yesterday. I never thought I'd see her again. I'd love to see her after this if I can?'

'Of course, Nigel, absolutely,' I said. We continued, to the cockatoos and African greys where we cleaned away half eaten fruit and veggies and gave them fresh new ones. 'We grow all their food here and have an amazing compost which leads to better food. It's a great setup.' He was really proud of it.

The birds seemed to get bigger and bigger; some were sitting on eggs in their nests and there was a great variety of birds. Way more than I would have expected Uncle Jerry to have had in his 'little pet shop.' And even though they were in cages, they had plants surrounding them. It was the most incredible place I had ever been.

It was mine; this whole place was truly mine.

We had a lot of bowls to top up with water. Nigel showed me how they collected their own water. When we finished looking at the aviary, I said, 'Are there any other animals here?'

He nodded. 'We've got some farm animals, and chickens, dogs, and pigs, but we don't do a lot of breeding of those.'

'What do you do with them?' I wanted to ask so many questions as it was all fascinating. But I didn't want to give my game plan away.

'We use the pigs, sheep, cows, chickens and their eggs as our food source. We are self-reliant out here. As you know, we harvest our water; grow our fruit and veggies. We even have solar power. Our trees bear fruit throughout the year.'

He handed me an apple, and I started eating it.

'Jerry was great at preserving the fruit, so other than beer and the odd things like bread, flour, and sugar, we don't need to rely elsewhere for most foods. It's great being self-sufficient.' We walked to another area where he took out some celery sticks and started placing them in cages. 'There is another animal we breed. It's not one we are proud of, but we breed poodles,' he said as he rolled his eyes.

Nigel was more relaxed away from the others. I suspected his tension was caused by them.

He said, 'I love these animals – I think of them as my babies. I must admit, Bee, I'm worried about what will happen to my job.'

'I'm sure you will be fine,' I assured him.

I couldn't keep all these magnificent creatures alive on my own. Man alive, was I going to need someone who loved them to help me? When he was talking about animals, Nigel genuinely spoke with love. He had the animal connection that Uncle

Jerry and I had. I hadn't seen this from the other three men, they creeped me out.

Nigel went on telling me about the poodles and how they had special fur that's non-allergenic. Because of that, they mixed other breeds with poodles to make pets that people weren't allergic to. We went into a large blue shed that surprisingly didn't reek of dog. There were a lot of poodles in there, but they were crossed with other dogs. Nigel said, 'I'm not a dog man. I like Basil. That's about as far as it goes.'

'I love Basil,' I said.

'Basil loves you too, from what I can see.' He patted me on the head. I think he confused me with a dog.

I just smiled at him, and Basil was still at my feet.

'It's been nice chatting, Belinda, but I've gotta go and check on all my eggs.'

'Can I come with you? I'd love to see how you check on them.'

We checked the eggs and turned the ones that needed turning.

Finally, he said he was done and walked off, leaving me alone. I had got all that I would get out of Nigel - for now.

Chapter 4: What now?

Belinda

When I returned to the house a couple of hours later, my family were all sitting around playing cards.

Jerry had loved playing cards. I remembered him teaching me how to play poker when I was really young, so I joined in the game.

'What do you think will happen to this place?' Mum asked before dropping two cards.

'It's so peaceful,' Cindy added. 'Uncle Jerry must have loved living here. Bee, you are an animal freak. Bet you love it here too.'

'Peaceful,' Marmalade agreed. That sent giggles off around the room.

I nodded, not ready to tell them yet, but I rambled on about the animals, birds and poodles.

'I'm eager to know what's going on,' Uncle Charlie asked.

My stomach dropped. The last thing I wanted was to upset my family.

'We should all move here,' Sofie said.

'Not likely, it's nothing like the city,' Cindy swatted away a big blowfly.

My hands went to my heart. I had pictured her living with me.

'I'm going to call Brandon,' I needed to get away from the love and guilt in that room.

Marmalade flew behind me as I went. I ran down the hall to my room and tapped out Brandon's phone number. I got his recorded message. 'Brandon here – chances are I am training or playing hockey – send me a text.'

I left a message *'It's me – I just wanted to chat.'*

He was never there when I needed him. I threw my phone on my bed and stomped to the window. The sun dimmed behind a cluster of clouds. I had to face facts. Our relationship had reached its expiration date. I let out a long sigh. Really, it had been over for months. I'd just been clinging on, hoping for the best. 'It's all up to me - I have to solve this puzzle alone,' I told Marmalade.

'Not alone,' Marmalade squawked.

She was right. I'd have help once the others knew.

'Good girl,' I said, rubbing her neck.

'Good girl. Love you,' she replied.

Somehow, she always said the right thing.

Mum often struggled to pay the mortgage. We could sell the house at home and move to the Manor.

I went to explore the rooms in our wing. Some were so dusty I didn't think anyone had been in them for years. If we moved here, Mum could work on the business. She was good with accounts. If Mum said no, then at sixteen, I could possibly legally live alone. I'd need to investigate that. I needed to spend some time with the other three workers, but I was fairly sure I was keen to keep Nigel on to run the place. I had almost finished school. Would Mum let me do the rest of the year via correspondence?

That would be the life.

All these thoughts and questions ran through my mind while I continued to explore. As I entered a room upstairs, I saw Mum's bags and was so focused on them I hadn't realised I wasn't alone.

'Hey,' a voice behind startled me.

I jumped.

'What's with you?' It was Cindy.

'Just having a look around. Look at this huge place. I would have loved to stay here when Uncle Jerry was alive. I always thought he lived in a little run-down cottage somewhere, not a mansion.'

'Looks like he was rich,' she said.

Money hadn't crossed my mind till then. My mouth dropped open as I stared at Cindy. I'd only thought about the animals.

'Rich?'

'What's with you, you're acting weird?' Cindy frowned.

'Can you keep a massive secret?' I had to tell someone; I was gonna burst hiding this secret.

'Shhhh secret,' Marmalade shrieked.

'Seriously, you're asking me that? Of all people, me! Spill. What's up?'

'Uncle Jerry has left all this to me: the house, business, and all his belongings!'

It took her a minute to say anything. She sat there, her face frozen. 'Why you? I can't believe that.' We sat down on the bed. 'Not our Mums?'

I shook my head. 'No, just me. That's what Mr Wade said. And I need to sort out the business, and the men who live here, plus the animals. Oh Cindy, there are so many amazing animals.'

'Too much responsibility,' she said, reaching out and holding me.

I let go of a breath. She understood.

I reached over to pat Marmalade and kiss her beak.

'Want to come live here with me?'

'What about school?' she replied.

'You go to school to get a job or start a business. Looks like I have one. We can learn skills on the job.'

Deep down, I knew Cindy and the twins would come to stay in the holidays, but Cindy would get bored if she lived here with me. She didn't have my passion for animals.

'For sure! As long as that hot helper stays! I would love to roll around in the hay with him.'

'Jacinda!' I laughed, throwing a pillow at her.

Not at all serious, that's all she thought about, boys, boys, boys!

Then she started laughing and flopped back to lie on the bed.

I flopped down beside her, and we both looked at the ceiling. 'What?' I said.

'The twins will be so jelly.'

We both laughed again.

'What's going on in here?' Mum checked on us.

I sat up, suddenly serious. 'Mum, please come in and sit down,' I said. 'I have something to tell you. I don't want to upset you, but earlier on—'

'You could never upset me,' Mum interrupted with a smile. Cindy sat up as Mum came to sit between us.

'Mr Wade, he took me for a walk and—'

'Yes, what was that all about?' she interrupted me again.

'Well, that's what I'm trying to tell you if you'd stop interrupting me.'

'Sorry,' she said, and she mockingly locked her lips shut.

'He said he had come to do the will reading, but it only involved me.'

I stopped talking at that point. Let it sink in. Hopefully, she would guess, and that would be easier than telling her.

We sat there in silence for what felt like a long time.

'So, he left you something?' she finally asked.

I nodded.

'And Mr Wade told you.'

Again, I nodded.

'This house?' she asked.

I nodded.

'The business?'

I nodded.

'Everything?'

'Yip'

'You are too young to drive.' Cindy started nodding, too. 'All of this, his money, everything he left to you. You own a house, have staff and a business now? You are only sixteen. What was he thinking?' She stood and started pacing.

Marmalade flew over to Mum, which was rare. 'We'll be okay,' she squawked.

Mum patted Marmalade. 'He was thinking you are the best person to run this business. He just died earlier than he hoped. He was always preparing you to look after his animals, wasn't he?'

I nodded.

'He was,' Marmalade added.

'He told me it excited him you were going to vet school. In two years, this would all make sense. Oh, the others,' Mum said. 'What will they say?'

'Yes,' said Cindy. 'That's what we were laughing about.'

'I will share any money with everyone,' I said.

'No,' Mum said. 'If you have the money, you may need it for the business. We need to be smart, love. We will get Mr Wade to come back in a couple of days and officially read the will to everyone.'

'Yes, that's what I asked him to do.'

'Great minds think alike,' Mum touched the bed and looked around the room. Her room now if she wanted to stay. 'Cindy, till then we need to make comments about how close Uncle Jerry and Belinda were,' Mum said.

'Sounds like a plan,' Cindy agreed.

'And I need to look into the business. If he has no money and hasn't paid his bills or if the Manor was mortgaged through the roof, we need to know.' Mum had turned on her business mode.

'Mr Wade said last week they found out something was wrong with the accounting, and just when Uncle Jerry started looking into it, suddenly he died.'

'Ok, I'll look into that too. The animals, you need to find out as much as you can about them, Bee,' Mum said to me.

'Nigel, the tall thin man, gave me a tour today, but he left one shed out. He said it had dangerous chemicals in there.'

'When you go out and about, I want you both together,' Mum stood up off the bed and looked out the window 'Wow, all of this is ours. What will we do?'

'I want to move here, Mum. It's paradise.'

Marmalade flew back to me. 'Paradise.'

'Got to say it sounds nice, waking to this every morning.' She turned from the window. 'Don't tell your father.'

'Never. I don't talk to him. He would just want to smoke and drink it all away.'

'He's not that bad,' Mum said, defending him.

'Mum, he stole ten thousand dollars from you and spent it all on one weekend in Rotorua.'

'Some of that money went on a tattoo of us.'

'Are you sure you want that man to have our faces tattooed on him, instead of food on our table?'

'Sorry, Bee, he was in the wrong. I just don't want you to be angry with him. He loves you in his own weird way. Let's change the subject, love. I don't want to get upset. What are they doing?' Mum asked, looking out the window not at the country view but at the men in the shed.

I hated it when Dad got Mum down, so I let her change the subject. Lucky Aunty Carol wasn't with us. She hated Dad even more than I did.

'That's the shed they said I can't go into,' I pointed. 'They were moving stock around by the looks of it. You stay here and watch. I'll go down there and see what they're doing.'

'Sure,' Mum said, 'go together and don't get separated.'

I left Marmalade with Mum, but Basil woke up from where he'd been sleeping by Uncle Charlie, and he followed us. We ran down to the aviary, and it didn't take long for us to run into Nigel.

'Whatcha doing?' I asked.

He looked flustered, like I'd caught him with his hand in the cookie jar.

'Umm, just moving some lizards around,' he said.

'Oh cool. Can I see?'

'Maybe later. This one is nocturnal and can't see the daylight. You should go back to the house.'

'Nah,' I said. 'I need to show Cindy around this place. She has no idea how amazing it is.'

'Okay, well, you should see the birds,' he said, pointing to the enormous building surrounded by trees and vines.

We skipped off. I knew the birds were to the right, but I turned left.

'The other way,' Nigel said, turning around to watch us.

'Okay,' I said.

We went into the bird aviary and observed the men from there. They were moving a lot of boxes. Jason dropped a crate and Murray, as good as, showed his teeth and growled at him.

'Sorry boss,' Jason said, picking it up.

Cindy saw the guy she liked and she ran over to him, her hair flying behind her. Damion lapped up Cindy's attention, laughing along with her feeble jokes. As she distracted him, I tried to investigate what he was carrying. It sounded like it was hissing. He hoisted a bulky canvas bag on his shoulder, slinging it behind his body as though he were trying to keep it out of sight. The fabric rippled. There was something moving inside it. I thought I heard a quiet hiss coming from it. Whatever it was, it had Basil barking and running in circles, all distressed.

Any time I had seen Basil around animals, he had been good with them. So, it made me curious about what animal was in there. But Basil was not happy, so we left.

'Cindy,' I called, 'look at this bird. It's amazing.'

Cindy glanced in my direction, then turned back to Damion. She gave him a wide smile. 'Okay,' she said to him, 'see you at tea. Don't let me down.'

Damion laughed. 'Promise.' He lifted three fingers in the air, making the scouts' honour sign.

'Oh, what is your favourite colour?' she called back to him as we left.

He looked puzzled. 'Green, I guess.'

'Okay, I'll wear green for you the next time you see me.' She winked.

She came into the bird aviary with me. I stood for a moment with my hands on my hips, shaking my head at her.

'What?' she said, glaring at me.

'You are such a flirt.' I laughed. 'The animal in the bag scared Basil. He needs to settle.' I scratched Basil's neck.

'Poor Basil,' she said, calming down too, 'but Damion is *so* hot.'

'And dodgy,' I added, raising my eyebrows.

'So, I have to ask you the big question,' she started.

'You want a pet?' I asked.

She laughed. 'No, but if I change my mind, I know where to go.'

'So, what do you want? Your wish is my command.'

'Do you have anything green that I can borrow?' she asked.

'Of all the things to ask,' I laughed. 'Sure, I've got a keep New Zealand beautiful tee-shirt that's green.'

'I guess it will have to do.' Cindy sighed, and we started wandering through the aviary, looking at the birds.

'Are you really wanting to move here? What about school, Daisy and most importantly Brandon? You two have been a couple forever.'

'Brandon talks about our future, but never past graduation.' I pursed my lips. I was trying not to think about our future, but I needed to face it. 'He wants to travel and has never talked about me traveling with him. Plus, he's just too obsessed with what everyone else thinks about him. Wanting me to look matchy with him or have me hanging off his arm at this event or that. He has not taken the time to just enjoy us. I don't think he even sees me as more than just his accessory now.'

'Sorry to hear that. You do make a beautiful couple.'

'Shut up!' I jokingly hit her. Brandon was the best-looking guy I'd ever seen. I couldn't believe it when he asked me out two years ago. He tried so hard to win me over. I didn't want a boyfriend, but he kept leaving notes in my school locker with cute puppy cartoons that he'd drawn himself. And his eyes were so puppy-dog that I couldn't resist him for long. Sadly, it had been a long time since he'd made any effort, and I'd later found out that he'd paid Tommy Watson to draw the puppies, not done by Brandon after all. I was too young to be stuck with a guy who didn't seem that interested. The one emotion Brandon still showed towards me was jealousy. He wouldn't let other guys talk to me. Even though I was only chatting, not flirting. Yes, I wanted to be able to have males as friends and being single did appeal to me.

After a long silence I said, 'Daisy, I would miss, but she can come visit.' I'd been contemplating my life's direction. While Cindy had probably been thinking about Damion.

The sun descended in the sky while we sat looking at the birds. The aviary was full of colourful birds. Some had a few orange feathers; Marmalade was the only fully orange bird there at all. Nigel was so excited seeing her, which was weird. I wondered if Marmalade still had a bond with any birds in there.

Looking around, I took in a big breath, smelling the fresh country air as I picked two apples from the closest tree. I gave one to Cindy. 'We could live this blissful life together.'

'Dinner Prep.' Aunty Carol was calling us, so we walked towards her.

'I need you two to come help me pick dinner,' Mum said, walking over to us.

'Charlie and Murray have gone off to the home-kill freezer to choose meat,' she told us as we walked over to the garden.

I picked an enormous raspberry from a row of healthy vines in the garden. 'I always thought Uncle Jerry bought the berries he gave us at Christmas.'

'Me too.' The gardens were ginormous, well maintained, and I didn't even know what half the vegetables were. It even had its own irrigation system set up from rainwater tanks, and a big glasshouse. Mum's eyes popped.

Chapter 5: Garden
Belinda

'This is the best garden I've ever seen,' Mum sung out. She was always looking at gardens in magazines. 'Okay, I could live here,' Mum said under her breath. 'We will move up soon. Need to see if you can study vet school by correspondence.'

I hugged her and wiped my eyes. 'This is paradise. You are amazing, Mum.'

I turned to Cindy 'Will you come for all the holidays?'

'Try and stop me,' she said.

I couldn't hide my grin then.

'What's going on here?' Cindy's mum asked as we arrived back inside.

'Just can't believe Uncle Jerry and this place. So much about him we didn't know. He came into our lives, but we never went into his.'

'We touched his life so much,' Sofie said, subtly moving her hand near her heart.

'Yeah, look at all of our art around the house,' Lily said.

'Especially your art, Bee. There is one of your paintings in almost every room,' Sofie added.

'Yeah,' Cindy said, 'Bee and Uncle J had a special bond. Do you know Uncle J drove down and back in one day just to go to grandparents' day and other school events for her? They saw him a lot more than we did.'

'Wow! We never knew that' Lily said.

'We came to visit him too, but we never came to his house, just to cafes, or the beach.'

'I didn't know you saw him more than we did,' Aunty Carol said.

'He gave us all our pets, too. Cause Bee and he shared a love for animals,' Mum said.

'They sure do. Did you see that giant birdcage? We thought of you when we saw it,' Sofie said.

I laughed. 'It's called an aviary. That's where we were earlier. I could just sit there all day long. It's amazing.'

'Yeah, you are definitely at home here,' Lily said.

'It's my paradise, that's for sure.'

'Uncle used to preserve the food. Some of the fruit is going to go off soon. We should try to pick and preserve, or freeze some fruit if we get a chance,' I added.

'I wonder how big the freezer is?'

'Have you not seen it?' Sofie said.

'Oh my, quick, come with us,' Lily added.

Cindy and I followed the twins till we saw a gigantic garage that was a giant walk-in freezer on one side, a giant fridge on another and a pantry in-between. That's where Uncle Jerry's preserves were. Followed by the twins, I got a couple of jars of apples for making apple crumble, which was his favourite, and that's what I would make for dessert in his honour.

There were many animal foods in bulk, too. The freezer had frozen bugs and other pet food. I took a photo as I would google some of them later. I had so much to learn. What if the men leave when they find out the business is not theirs? I started to cry, in a panic about how I was going to do this. I couldn't do it.

'What's wrong Bee?' Lily asked. She had no idea of my burdens. Would I lose them when they found out?

'I wish that I had stayed here when Uncle was alive, that he was here showing us all this.' I lied.

'Oh Bee,' they said in turns while the other hugged me. They stayed for a while but were not invested, so were not interested. The twins left when they thought I was emotionally stable again, but I wanted to see more and Cindy stayed supporting me.

I took many photos on my phone so I could look up the foods and find out which animals they were for. As Cindy and I looked at the general storage, we could see dust had been disturbed recently. We moved some cartons, and, in the back, found boxes with words on them written in a foreign language. Cindy and I looked at each other. 'What language do you think this is?' Cindy asked.

I shrugged. 'I'm more interested in why they're shoved back here, where no one will find them.'

Cindy opened a box and inside was a smaller sealed box with danger written in red on it. We took photos of them and put them carefully back where we found them. We opened one, and it had something inside that looked like mashed wood chips.

'Put your hand in there and see what it is,' Cindy said.

'Are you kidding? What if there's something in there that bites or stings?'

As we looked, something in the box moved and we both jumped back.

'Oh.'

'What the....!'

'No,' she said, quickly closing the box. And just in time.

The door at the other end of the freezer scraped open, and Cindy and I ducked behind a stack of boxes out of sight as a couple of men came in. 'Jerry didn't know what was going on and with luck, his relatives will be gone in a couple of days, and we can get back to business as normal.' That sounded like Murray. Then Jason's voice replied. 'But what if they stumble on to the cargo?'

'If anything changes, we will deal with it then. We have done all we can do now. Just do your job and stop talking or we will get overheard!' The first man snapped.

We stayed in silence, hiding in the shed for five more minutes after they left, then Cindy turned to me and said, 'They are up to something, aren't they?'

'Yes,' I replied. 'I'm scared that they're doing something illegal. I don't trust them at all and hate to say this, but I'm worried that they might have done something awful to Uncle Jerry.'

Cindy shook her head, 'I can't believe Damion would do anything illegal. Maybe they can explain what they're doing here.'

'I'm going to get to the bottom of whatever is going on.'

'I have no doubt you will.' She laughed. 'Maybe they are illegally farming maggots.' Deciding to keep my suspicions to myself for now, we strolled back to the kitchen slowly, where I washed my hands and got stuck in helping Mum make a salad for dinner. It was like a Christmas dinner, everyone under each other's feet, no one knowing what job to do, resulting in us finding out that two lots of potatoes had been prepared.

Sophie let out a whine. 'Look at this enormous pot of spuds! I've been standing here for hours getting shriveled hands from all this peeling and now I find out Mum already did some.'

'Potatoes for breakfast,' Cindy and I said together.

Mum and I grew a few veggies at home, and Mum loved gardening, but this meal was all made from the land! I was looking forward to eating it. Especially the apple crumble.

'Bee – can you please show me the poodles?' Lily asked as the potatoes boiled away and that gave us some free time. I looked at Cindy 'I have a book to read for school.'

Lily and I traipsed over to the poodle shed.

'Oh my gosh – they are so cute,' she said. We both climbed a barrier and sat down in a pen with 8 puppies, black, white and a combination. They were all cute, but I didn't have the connection I had with the birds, but Lily did. I smiled, watching her with them. Eventually, she found a favourite. It jumped up on her. 'Do you think if this place is left to us, I can have a puppy?' she asked.

I knew she could if she could get Uncle Charlie to agree.

'Would that be your pick?' I asked as the dogs calmed down and the white poodle, she'd been patting's eyes fluttered closed.

'Definitely.'

'What would you name him?'

'Hikarere, Māori for snow.'

'Snow gets muddy too,' I laughed, noting which distinguishable marks Hikarere had.

The door opened, and Murray froze in the door watching us. 'What the fuck are you doing? Don't play with the bloody stock. You interfering little....' he stopped. Pissed off Murray was terrifying, his neck pulsing as I swallowed my fear.

'Sorry Murray,' I said, standing.

'Sorry,' Lily followed shaking.

It was so quiet not even the puppies made a scratch. Murray ran his hand through his greasy hair and planted his fake smile on. 'I guess it's good for them to interact with humans – just please ask us before you play with the pets.'

Far..... Did he have bipolar or something? We walked out of the shed door and around the corner, leaving the now barking puppies and Murray alone.

I should have felt scared, but I pulled Lily into the empty bird aviary and burst into laughter. She followed. She and I looked between named labeled pictures of birds on the walls and the real feathered beauties trying to learn their names. Lily did it as a game – but it was more than that to me. An hour later, the whole family and the four workers we'd invited sat around an enormous table in a dining room that the twins had spent half the day cleaning.

Charlie had an idea to separate the four men at dinner so we could all get to know them. The only people happy with this arrangement were Cindy and Damion, who flirted throughout the meal. Murray was next to Lily and more than once I saw him look at her distastefully. Nigel and I talked bird breeds from across the table.

The apple crumble was the highlight of dinner and after that we all left for bed nice and early. We had a lot to think about before the funeral the next day. I fell asleep quickly but woke up at three in the morning and could not go back to sleep. The bird noises sounded different. I tiptoed out to see what was strange with the birds in the aviary. There wasn't a cloud in the sky, so it was easy to walk by the light of the moon, but that also meant I had to keep close to the side of the house amongst the bushes. If I could see my way clearly, it probably meant others could see me coming.

Marmalade had stayed asleep, her head tucked away in her feathers, but Basil had woken up and followed me. I thought all the birds in the aviary would be asleep, but some were awake, rustling and chirping in the foliage. I crept towards the back of the aviary, and found cages hidden there, containing kiwis. They were breeding kiwis. To sell? Surely not. I heard a morepork and had assumed it was from outside, but as I investigated, I found a morepork in a cage too.

If this was for conservation, I was all for it, but why be so secretive and why have them in small cages instead of larger ones? Why not build them a proper habitat?

I heard someone coming, so I hid behind a cage which held a bat. Nigel walked in carrying a full bowl of grubs and put one of the kiwis in a cage before leaving again. Oh, Nigel, what are you up to?

When he left, I took some videos and photos; I needed somewhere quiet to think, so I left the aviary and made my way to the chickens. I had so much going around in my mind. How was I going to find out what they were up to? And if these men were really doing something illegal, what was I going to do about it? This place was like a fairytale dream, and a scary nightmare, and not a lot in between.

I knew these workers were up to no good. On my land with my business. I knew I couldn't run the business without them, yet I was responsible for the farm. Could I get into trouble for what they'd been doing? I was still at school, just a kid, and my Mum knew business and accounting, but not animals.

But I couldn't trust these guys. I liked Nigel, but he appeared to be in on it, too. Whatever it was, it was up to me to make it right. After I had visited the chickens, I sat and pondered on everything, sitting on an old moss-covered bench chair outside the aviary.

At four-thirty in the morning, I saw Nigel walk in the shadows towards the aviary, so I followed him. Murray and Jason rushed from one shed to another, talking in hushed tones, but they were too far away for me to hear what they were saying.

Nigel went inside the aviary and sat with the birds. I didn't know what those men were up to, but one thing I knew for sure, Nigel loved those birds. He sat with them for an hour, talking to each one and patting them, while he changed their water and fed them.

As I sat on the mossy seat, I slowly drifted off to sleep. I awoke to Damion saying, 'Well, well, well, what do we have here?'

I sat up massaging my neck, not the most comfortable way to sleep. 'I can't believe I fell asleep.'

'When? How long have you been here? All night?' his puzzled gaze reached me.

'No, I'm not sure of the time. I got up early, but I can't have been here long. It's so beautiful,' I added.

'Have you seen anyone else?' he asked, looking around.

'No, just birds. They make me feel so relaxed, listening to them. So relaxed, I must have fallen asleep. Today's the day we bury the man who was like my poppa. It's all very surreal.'

'Were you that close?' he asked me.

'Yeah, you have seen that lounge inside?' I asked, with my left hand on my gold bangle that Uncle Jerry had given me for my 16th birthday.

'Yeah.'

'Well, I did all the paintings on the wall. I knitted the throw, I made the cushions, the candles. It's like my personal art gallery. So weird! I can't believe he didn't just box it all up. There's more of my stuff in there than at home.'

Damion appeared genuinely surprised.

'What about the other girls?'

'There are a few of their things around, but between you and me, I think they frustrated him. They had nothing in common, but he and I were always close. He taught me all about animals and I'm going to be a vet, or somehow work with animals when I grow up. I just love them and it's all his influence.'

Damion sat beside me and listened to my rambling. 'Every year for my birthday, he would get me a pet or animal book, or toys for our pets. After Marmalade, Mum had said no more pets, but he had told me he was getting me a special dragon for my birthday this year. That was three months ago, but we haven't seen him since then.'

'Oh, I know which one it is. I will bring it to you later if you like.'

'You have no idea how special it would be to have my last ever gift from Uncle Jerry.' My eyes filled with tears.

I would treasure that dragon always.

'Sorry I made you cry,' he said as I wiped my tears away. 'Tell me about Cindy.'

'Oh Cindy,' I teased him and smiled.

'How old is she?'

'Old enough,' I said, 'and how old are you?'

'Twenty-two,' he said.

'Maybe she's not old enough then. Do you normally go for girls six years your junior?' I like that he liked her, but there was something creepy about him.

'Six years,' Damion said, 'Wow! Maybe not.'

'Want to know her hobbies?'

'Why not?' he said.

'Well, it used to be basketball, swimming, and shopping with her mates, but now it's you, you and you!' I laughed.

He laughed too. I was about to say, seriously she's just flirting with you, please leave her alone but just then Cindy turned the corner with a bowl of berries from the garden. We both stopped laughing. It might have seemed like we were talking about her, which we were. She looked upset and started to walk away. Damion stood up.

'Hey Cindy,' I called out. I didn't want her upset with me. She's all I had. 'Someone was just asking for the down-low on you.'

She turned around, swaying her hips and running her hands through her freshly washed hair.

'I hear you like basketball. Me too,' he said, then he turned back to me and winked.

'This seat's warm, Cindy. Come sit. I'm off to have a shower.'

As I reached the corner, I turned and saw them holding hands. I hoped Damion was as nice as he seemed, and that Cindy wasn't getting in over her head.

Chapter 6: Funeral

Belinda

Uncle Jerry always told me he liked red, so I wore a puffy, bold red dress to his funeral. If I added wings, I would have looked like one of the bright red birds from the aviary.

It surprised me how many people were at Uncle Jerry's funeral. It was as if the whole town had showed up to pay their respects. Family, work, and his country club. The club where people knew all about our family.

'Are you Belinda?' a lady in a black suit asked Cindy.

Cindy shook her head and pointed at me.

'Are you Belinda?' a man in a black suit and white tee-shirt asked me.

'Yes.' I smiled politely.

'Your uncle spoke so highly of you.'

'Thanks.' What was I meant to say? Who are you? Or I didn't know. Nothing else felt

right, so thank you was what I said to most
of them. I was flattered that Uncle Jerry had
talked to his friends about me.

We four girls started the service singing,
How Great Thou Art for him one last time.
Every year at Christmas we put on a concert
and Uncle Jerry loved that song. I knew
he would have been pleased. I also read a
poem I had written for him.

'*Your heart has stopped, but you go
on in mine forever, a beating shadow
that remains, reminding me of all the
life lessons you taught me, the jokes we
shared...*'

When I got overwhelmed halfway
through, Mum finished reading the poem for
me as I wept beside her.

'*Songs we sang, forever with me. Love
you Uncle Jerry.*'

After the funeral service, our parents
asked us girls to walk around offering club
sandwiches, little mince pies, and quiches
to everyone. I spent more time talking
to strangers. I was interested in all the
people; who they were and their connection
to my uncle. There were people of all
ethnicities and ages. The real estate lady

was working tastelessly approaching the church attendees for business – she and her inappropriate leopard skin jacket better not be selling my manor. I saw a group of people my age, but I never got to talk to them, but the twins got to. I hadn't spoken to Cindy since this morning, as Damion had been next to her the whole time. Not holding hands, but close enough. I guess he thought six years was not too big an age gap. I still disagreed. There were so many faces, and they were looking at me. I kept catching their eyes and looking away, but there was a boy whose eyes I didn't turn from. He didn't turn from my glance, either. I recognised him as the boy playing rugby at the beach the day we first drove through town. He started walking towards me.

'Sorry about your uncle,' he said shuffling his feet. 'He was a great man with a great heart.'

'Hi, how did you know my uncle?' I manage to get out. I was tripping over my words but didn't know why.

'He's friends with my uncle, and I often listened to them talking about animals which are my passion.'

'He taught me everything I know about animals. I love him so much,' I felt the corners of my mouth raise. He was so full of knowledge; I love that he helped others too.

'Do you like the animals? What's your favourite?' He took a step closer to me. His aftershave was subtle but irresistible, I wanted to lean in closer to pick out the scents in it.

I was about to reply, but Mr Wade interrupted us. 'Belinda, I need to introduce you to somebody.'

I started to breathe normally again as Mr Wade pulled me away before I could even ask what the boy's name was. I was drawn to keep talking to him. It was a lot more fun talking to him than the adults Mr Wade introduced me to. Mr Wade, between mouthfuls of cucumber sandwich, introduced me to Mrs McLaren, the accountant. I called Mum over to meet her, too.

'Hi, can we come to your office tomorrow afternoon?' Mum asked.

'Yes, certainly. Would three o'clock suit you?' Mrs McLaren checked her phone calendar.

'Perfect.'

I turned to Mr Wade. 'Any chance you can come over to the house before then to officially read the will? I have told Mum I would love you to read it to the family and staff, if that's okay?'

'Absolutely, love.' Mr Wade smiled at me.

'I will act surprised,' I said, putting on a fake surprised face.

He smiled. 'You remind me of Jerry.' He did a small chuckle. 'I hope we get to see more of you up here.'

'Me too,' I added. 'I love it here. I just wish Uncle Jerry were here to show me the ropes.'

'That had been the plan, Belinda.'

We were interrupted again, this time because it was time for our family to go to the cemetery.

As we stood at the graveside clinging to one another, I held myself together as much as possible. Still tears fell as Uncle Jerry was lowered into the ground, knowing his plan for me. I made him a silent promise: *I won't* let *you down.* I would sort out his workers, learn everything I could. I would make him proud of me and keep his business flowing legally.

Chapter 7: Kiwi

Belinda

Back at the house, I went to my room and lay down on my bed. A couple of family members came to see if I was all right, but I pretended to be asleep. I'd had enough of pretending to be strong. But I needed to gather strength for my next move. The next thing I knew, it was three in the morning again. I got up and went down to the birds. Wide awake, I wanted to arrive before Nigel to silently watch what he did. But he was already there.

'Hey,' I said, 'Whatcha doing?'

'Belinda!'

He jumped and dropped the bag of birdseed he was holding, spilling it all over the ground.

'What the—don't creep up on people like that!' he snapped, scrambling to clean up the mess. 'Are you trying to give me a heart attack?'

'You can just call me Bee. Is that a Kiwi?' I asked.

'Um yeah. '

'Is it sick?' I feigned naivety.

'Um, yeah,' he replied rubbing his neck unconvincingly.

'Can I help? I can't sleep.'

'Not surprised. You went to sleep early last night.' He laughed. 'We all stayed awake drinking for a few hours, even your cousins.'

'It was a distressing day.'

'Are you going home today?' he asked as I went and sat next to him and the kiwi.

'Nah, Mr Wade's coming to do the will reading. Maybe the next day. I don't know how much stuff Mum and Aunty will have to sort. Bills to pay and all that.'

'Murray pays all the bills,' he said.

'Oh well, I guess whatever they need to sort. I'm hoping to attempt to make some preserves today.'

'That's a great idea. Jason is the man to see. He can tell you which trees need picking at the moment.'

'Do you all have job areas?' I asked as we walked around, topping up food and filling water bowls.

'Yeah.'

'Let me see if I can guess.'

'Okay,' he laughed.

'You are the birdman?'

'Yip.'

'And Jason is the caretaker, stock and garden man?'

'Yip, and Jerry was too,' he added.

'Loverboy, a.k.a. Damion, he's reptiles?'

'Spot on.'

'And Murray, he's livestock and general boss?'

'Yip.'

'There's one thing I don't get.'

He tensed up.

'Why aren't you guys married? I haven't seen any girls around here?'

His tight expression relaxed, he let out a sigh, almost a laugh. Was he relieved by the simplicity of my question?

'Well, Damion is a pretty boy and has had half the town's women after him, but he's taken by Cindy at the moment. Murray's madly in love, but he only sees his lover in his reflection.' We both laughed.

'So, he's all about him.'

'Yip,'

'Few people know this, but Jason and I are together.'

I frowned, confused. 'Together?' I was still unsure where he was going.

'He and I are, me and he,' Nigel said, tripping over himself. 'Oh,' I said, getting it, 'you are a couple?'

'Yeah, but we haven't told the others. Please say nothing.'

'No worries. I've got your back if you have mine.'

'Sure,' he said.

'So, I have so many more questions.'

'About the birds or Jason?'

'Both. Wings, do you clip them? And did you know you were gay before you met Jason?'

'Wait, wait, wait. I'm not gay. I'm just into Jason. Before him, it was always women I liked, but there was something about Jase and well he's here. It's convenient.'

'Okay, okay,' I said, putting my hands over my ears. Clearly, he hadn't emerged from the closet completely.

'And I clip some wings, but not others.'

I laughed. 'That wasn't helpful at all.'

Nigel and I chatted until the sun lit the land.

'What's going on here?' Murray asked changing this light air, he reeked of stale cigarette smoke.

'I couldn't sleep,' I replied holding in a cough. That smelly man was gross but he had the knowledge that I needed, so I couldn't piss him off. I sure had an urge to kick him high between his legs.

'She's just tagging along. She has a thing about birds,' Nigel added.

'I see that,' Murray said, looking at the African Grey perched on my shoulder.

'That bird won't go to anyone but Jerry and me. She was a favourite of your great uncle once removed, or whatever he was,' Nigel said.

'He was basically my granddad. Aside from Uncle Charlie, he was the most constant man in my life.' I added, 'Dad took off before I started at kindergarten, and

Jerry's brother passed away before I was born.'

'Oh,' Nigel said.

'What are you doing now?' I asked Murray.

The question took him by surprise. 'I'm going to feed the sheep.'

'Can I come?' I stood up and put the African grey back in her cage.

'I guess I have to say yes, don't I?'

'Yes, please,' I said, as I winked at Nigel.

Murray gave Nigel an evil glare before glancing at the kiwi. 'Come on then, kiddo, let's leave Nigel to the birds.'

Chapter 8: Murray

Belinda

As we walked off, I said to Murray, 'Isn't Nigel amazing helping to look after that injured kiwi? He's a hero.'

'That he is,' Murray said, smiling and looking more relaxed.

Murray was easier to talk to after that and we walked around paddocks and climbed fences checking on the herd of fifty cows, a mob of sixty-eight sheep, and seven goats; it was a pleasant morning for it. Murray told me how a home kill truck came to carry out the killing of the livestock. And a shearer came to shear the sheep.

'Uncle always gave me wool for my knitting; I didn't know it was from his sheep. 'I pointed to my jumper. 'So, which one of you sheep helped me with this jumper? Thanks for your wool,' I said to all the sheep with a laugh. Murray looked at me like I was crazy. At least he didn't see me as a threat, yet. The next big paddock had a cluster of trees in the middle. Several of the sheep were huddled under the trees, chewing away at the grass.

'You are just like Jerry,' Murray said, watching Basil and me with a crinkle at the corner of his eyes. 'I reckon he loved animals more than people. He talked to them too.'

'Thanks. That's the best compliment I've had all day.'

'It's only five in the morning.' He gave a small slightly strained chuckle.

'A great start to the day, wouldn't you say?' I grinned back at him. 'Who milks the cows?'

'The neighbours. They'll come soon for the cattle.'

'That's smart,' I said.

'Thanks,' he said. 'I set it up.' The way Murray gave himself self-praise, smoked and had tattoos, he reminded me of Dad. I wonder if that's why I didn't like him. I would hate it if Dad ever found out about this place.

'Do you milk the goats?' I pointed to the goats milling around in the next paddock.

'No,' he said. 'We used to breed goats. These were the best breeders. We have been thinking about it again as we have five goats that are all different bloodlines.'

'So, do you walk around the farm every morning like this?'

'Yes, I check on farm maintenance and animal well-being. Holes in fences, sick animals—that sort of thing.'

'So today they are all good?'

'Yeah, except for the horse, she is broken-hearted since Jerry passed.'

'I haven't seen the horse.'

'She's in the stable.'

'Can we see her?' A horse! I own a horse?

'After the chickens.' He led me over to a tractor parked by the shed and helped me climb up. Together, we rumbled out on the worn track. I held on so tight my knuckles started turning white as we made our way along to the chicken coop. I couldn't talk when we were on the tractor, as I was busy gripping on tight and would have had to yell over the engine.

'So, tell me about all those chickens,' I said as we got down from the tractor. 'How many eggs do they lay?'

'Lots of eggs. We sell them and other products at the farmer's markets, which is the first Sunday of the month.' He kicks the dirt as we walk. 'We split the money, and we all have a holiday from our shares of what we make at the markets.'

'Where do you go?' I asked.

'Overseas, different places.'

'Cool.'

'I'm due to go to Hawaii in two weeks,' he said.

'Do the others go at the same time?'

'Last month the young buck went to Thailand, and the other two are going to Bali next month, which will be the first time two of us have gone away at one time, but we all know each other's jobs so we can carry the other's workload.'

This was all helpful knowledge for me. If only one man was dodgy, I could just get rid of that one and still run the business with help from the other three. Individually, they all came across as nice guys. Which of them was screwing Uncle over?

What was Murray's story?
Was he a good guy or a criminal?
The boss of a gang?
Or a combination of them all?
And how was I going to find out?

Chapter 9: Ruby

Belinda

'Can we see the horses now? I love horses!'

The stables were on the other side of the fence. I had seen the building and thought it was the neighbour's.

They were huge, with an enormous area for the horses to run and jump as well. OMG, all of this was mine, too. We walked inside the shed, and I could see there was room for at least ten horses, but only four were inside in their own little stalls. There was a tidy room with horse gear, again enough for ten horses. The stable was wooden with forest green accents and the words Loveridge's stables on the building and equipment. It even had its own driveway.

'Why are there so many empty stalls?' I asked Murray. As he spoke to me, he topped up the horses' water and food. I soaked in everything he was doing so I could do it if he left Black Manor.

'Jerry was the horseman, but the attention needed by the other animals had taken over, so Jerry just had his favorite breeders left, and his favourite pet.'

As he said that, we reached the stall where there was a horse laying in the back corner facing a wall. I instinctively opened the gate and walked in. The mare was black, but with a white marking down her mane with a pink nose. I gently went and sat next to her. She responded as I slowly patted her mane and softly sung sweet Caroline. Uncle Jerry always sung Neil Diamond to me, maybe he did to her too. She licked my palm. I couldn't stop the grin from spreading across my face. In the stall with this horse, I felt like I was home. This was my home, and I would fight for it. I even loved the smell of the hay.

With eyebrows raised, Murray said, 'Her name is Ruby. I can't believe she is acting like that with you. Please don't get attached to her. She hasn't eaten for days, so I guess I will have to shoot her soon.'

He walked away to do something else, but I stayed with Ruby. No! He couldn't shoot her! I would get her to eat if it was the last thing I did. I stood up and got a handful of food and was back next to her, singing the whole time. She put her tongue out and ate a little. Murray returned glaring at me. 'Belinda, Ruby hasn't been this alert since Jerry died. I have work to do. Close the gates on your way out please,' and he walked off.

I had intended to follow him, but Ruby needed me more. Ruby picked some more crumbs from my hand. I stayed with her for the rest of the morning. I may have even fallen asleep. When my hunger pains exceeded my need to comfort Ruby, I kissed her on the head and told her I would be back. I loved how everyone said I reminded them of my uncle, and I hoped Ruby felt it, too.

As I got up, Ruby got up. She had a drink of water before she walked with me. Relief washed over me. I put a lead on her, and she followed me to the house. Uncle Jerry had paid for me to go to a horse camp once a year since I was old enough to go. I knew how to look after horses. My cousins had been a few times with me too. I couldn't wait to show them we had five horses. The twins were outside in the garden throwing a netball to each other. When they saw me approaching with Ruby, they ran to meet me.

'Where have you been? Mum was about to call the cops. Where did the horse come from?' Lily said, patting Ruby on the nose.

'We were so worried,' Sofie added, following her sister's lead and patting Ruby. 'And who's this beauty?'

'Oh, what time is it?' I patted my jeans pockets for my phone. Oops must have left it behind again.

'Two in the afternoon,' Lily told me.

'Oops.'

'Belinda!' Mum stormed out of the house and strode towards us. 'Thank goodness you're back. Mr Wade wants to read the will.' Her eyes put me in my place instantly. I should not have been late for this big moment.

'I'm sorry,' I said, 'So sorry.'

Everyone was gathered at the outside table, eyes on me. The four farm workers, my family, and Mr Wade. He winked at me.

'Sorry, I need some food.' I said as I tied Ruby up to a hitching post by the house that I had never noticed before.

'Hold up, I'll get you some,' Cindy said.

'Let me help,' Damion offered.

Quickly, I washed my hands while they got me a plate of food. I scrubbed longer than I needed to, trying to avoid the news that may break my family in two. When we were all seated outside at the long-oval picnic table, Mr Wade started the meeting. 'The will reading is going to be quick. Jerry has left everything: the house, land, business, the stock and all his assets to Belinda Loveridge.'

There was a moment of silence when everyone seemed to go rigid. Slowly they all turned to look at me. I tried not to squirm under the intensity of their gazes.

'Left it to Belinda?' Aunty Carol's eyebrows creased.

Mr Wade nodded. I was thankful to be the only one at the table with cutlery, because everyone else was looking like they wanted to throw a knife at me. I wanted to say something, anything, to defend myself. But I had done nothing wrong and whatever I said would sound defensive. I looked at Mum. She gulped and opened her mouth as if to say something, but then closed it again. Perhaps she decided it was better to say nothing than the wrong thing, too.

'We own some of the stock,' Murray said, abruptly rising to his feet. 'We were equal partners.'

'Mrs McLaren has all the documents, and she's in her office now and would like to go over everything with the four of you.'

'Belinda, she would like you and your mum to go in and see her, too.'

'That's not fair,' Lily said.

'We were just as related to him as she was, Mum,' Sofie added.

'I didn't ask for this,' I said, 'but I love animals.' I looked over at Ruby, tied up at the garden fence. Just then Ruby lifted her head and looked right at me.

'Did you do that?' Nigel asked, following my gaze.

'She's lovely, isn't she?'

'Are you an animal whisperer?' Nigel asked.

I gave Nigel half a smile.

'I'm going to sort this now!' Murray said, storming off.

'Why is he upset? He's not even family' Lily asked.

'He thought Jerry had no family and always talked about us five being equal business partners, so we thought the business would be given to us in shares,' Nigel explained. 'We have all treated this as our business for years, so this is disappointing, to tell you the truth.'

'The land and buildings were all owned by Jerry. As was the majority of the stock. The four workers perhaps invested in shares for the business and may be entitled to some of the business profits, but not the assets.' Mr Wade had done his investigating.

'We didn't know that' Nigel said glaring at Murray talking on his phone over by the sheds. Lots of things needed to be talked about. I planned to start a notebook so I could write down all the things I needed to learn and find out about.

'Is it legal to leave the business to a sixteen-year-old?' Charlie asked Mr Wade.

'Yes, her mother will be the executor of the will until she is older, but the will is clear and legal.'

'That's good to know,' Charlie said, then he came over to me and shook my hand. 'Congratulations, love, this property is right up your alley. We will support you with whatever you need.'

I cried in relief and hugged him. He was on my side; this just got a little easier.

'I didn't ask for this.'

'I know, love,' he said, kissing my cheek.

Aunty Carol got up and stiffly hugged me, too. The twins got up, but instead, they walked away. My heart sank at their cold response. But maybe they'd get over it in time. A brand-new ute skidded down the driveway as Murray left to sort the business out.

'We better get back to work. You are still paying us right, boss?' Nigel asked me.

I nodded, not really understanding any of it yet.

'Everything will work out,' Mum answered for me.

Slowly, in ones or twos, everybody left till it was just Mum and me.

'I think we should see that accountant in an hour after Murray has left,' she said.

'Yip, I think you're right. First, I need to take Ruby back to her stall.'

Ruby and I walked over to the stables. I'd settled her in, given her some fresh hay, and was just stroking her neck and whispering a quiet goodbye when Nigel and his boyfriend came into the shed. I leant closer to the horse, patting her gently as the men, unaware that I was there, started to talk. 'What are we gonna do?' Jason asked. He paced back and forth, flicking hay into the corners with his boot.

'Guess we will just ride the wave,' Nigel responded, his voice calm and soothing, like he was trying to settle a spooked horse.

'What about the extras?' Jason looked around but didn't see me.

'I guess we sell them,' Nigel shrugged.

'I hope Belinda and her family don't find out.'

'Jerry never knew what was going on under his nose, but these new people might be nosier. I'm tired of all this sneaking around. I want to live a normal life,' Nigel said. 'Without having to look over our shoulders all the time, and I want to be open about you.'

Jason shook his head. 'Don't think the others will go for that.' He looked down at the ground and shrugged. 'Well maybe.' He reached out to grip Nigel's shoulder. 'I'm over this *watching our backs* shit. We have a choice. It's hard to say what any of our futures are now. Maybe we can see this change as a new start.'

'Just calm down and ride the wave. Belinda is very much like Jerry, and I think she's gonna do well for the legitimate side of things, and I want to be a part of that. I've gotta see to some eggs. I'll catch you later.' Nigel gave his boyfriend a quick kiss after checking the coast was clear. Thankfully, he didn't see me.

As they came towards me, I walked again, so they thought I had just arrived.

'You'll be alright, Ruby,' I said. 'Oh, hi Nigel, a bit of a shock, isn't it? Sorry, I don't know what to say. Mum and I are going to Mrs McLaren's soon.'

'Good on you, Belinda. You'll do the right thing.'

'Thanks for your vote of confidence, Nigel. You've been a real help the last couple of days.' Ruby was doing so much better but still I didn't want to leave her cooped up and lonely in a dark stall, so I put her in the paddock. Once she was settled chewing grass contentedly beneath a shady oak, I left her and went to find Mum. She was in the kitchen prepping vegetables for dinner.

'Are you ready to go, Mum?' I asked, snagging an apple from the bowl on the bench.

She wiped her hands on a towel and took a set of keys from a hook beside the door. We made our way to the garage to find Uncle Jerry's car. Last time we'd seen him, he'd been driving a BMW, but I remembered he'd also had an older vehicle he referred to as a classic. We met Nigel at the garage door.

'I've just come to get the three-wheeler,' he said as the door rumbled open.

Light spilled into an enormous room with not two cars, but many cars.

'Wow.' I turned to Nigel. 'Which one is Uncle Jerry's?'

Nigel laughed. 'None of them!'

'Oh,' I said, my eyes wrinkling. Where was his BMW? And who owned all these? Murray?

'They're all yours now.' He opened his arms dramatically and chuckled.

'What!' as in what? 'I don't even have my license.'

'About time to get it, don't you think?' he said.

Mum laughed.

Mum still went to Jerry's old BMW, and we drove that into town to see Mrs McLaren. I was beginning to know the road, the curves and hills, and the spots where there were quick glimpses of the beach. I loved the beach.

'Please help me with the money side Mum, I can learn the animal side.'

'Tell you what, how about you focus on the animals for now and I will sort out the finances, but when they are in order, I would like to show you them as well. You don't just have one strength. Belinda, please remember that.'

When we got to Mrs McLaren's, we found out that we had enough money to pay

Murray and the others out. Uncle Jerry was seriously loaded.

The twins had said earlier that if they got money or half the Black Manor, they would sell it and go on a worldwide holiday.

'Mum, I want to pay off Uncle Charlie's mortgage, and set up my cousins financially, please.'

'Yes, I knew you would.' Mum smiled at me. 'I'm immensely proud of you, Bee.'

I was really upset when I heard others talking about selling the farm, and I guess that's why Uncle Jerry left it to me, knowing I would not want to sell it. With the amount of money sitting in the account, I was also glad that Mum was an accountant and that she knew what to do with money, and a little excited that she would teach me too. She was right. I had strengths, and now I got to use everything I had learnt in school, in real life.

I was still waking up early in the morning, so the next day I decided to walk a different way around the farm. It was a rainy morning. I looked around and found some rain jackets hanging on the hook. The smallest raincoat was far too big for me, but I slipped it on and rolled the sleeves up, so it only covered part of my hands. I bypassed gumboots in favour of my pink and white sneakers. I'd put them on to wash and dry once I got back. Outside, I walked in the opposite direction from the big sheds towards the front of the farm, Basil bounding along with me. I found a small paddock which had no livestock, but it was still a very useful one and by far the most beautiful I had ever seen. I counted the rows of sage green shrubs, one, two, three—right up to twenty-seven. Twenty-seven rows of what I assumed would be lavender by Christmas time. I thought back to the lavender gifts I'd often received from Uncle Jerry.

All these years, the gifts that he had given us had obviously come from this beautiful place. I imagined coming back in summer, laying in the field, reading a book, simply daydreaming, smelling lavender and no doubt listening to buzzing bees. Was there such a thing as lavender honey? Lavender was my favourite flower, and I knew it had so many benefits, but not what the benefits were. Yet another thing I needed to look into and learn.

Walking the different route, I found a shed I'd not seen before. I approached the shed slowly. Unlike the rest of the farm buildings, which were well maintained, it looked derelict, nestled amongst a mass of scraggly mānuka, almost as if it was trying to hide. The olive paint was peeling off the boards, the wood of the windowsills visible through the ancient layers of shabby green trim. I took a quick look around to make sure no one was nearby and tried the rusty door handle. The door didn't budge. Damn. It was locked.

What was in that shed? Was it one of the sheds I was warned not to go into? I peered through the windows and inside were large colourful frogs in cages. What were frogs doing in a farm shed in New Zealand? That couldn't be legal! How did they get there? Who was responsible for this? Nigel warned me some sheds were dangerous. Had he lied to me? What was his involvement in it all?

I needed to find out why there were giant colourful frogs on the farm and who put them there, and how deep Nigel's involvement was. Surely native frogs were in greens and browns.

I ran back to the house to grab my phone so I could search for native frogs, but before I could reach my room, Mum called my name. 'Bee, get dried, quickly.'

I had the world's quickest shower and got into dry clothes; I sat at the dining room table with Mum and Mrs McLaren. We had to comb through the accounts as I ate fresh yellow yolked eggs on toast.

'You need to know this too, Bee. I can't do it alone,' Mum said.

Did she know how much work there was on the farm? I couldn't tell her about the frogs in front of Mrs McLaren, that was for sure.

Time flies when you are having fun, but when you are balancing spreadsheets and paying invoices, it came to a near standstill.

Just as I thought we might have completed the paperwork, Mrs McLaren told us we had to go to the bank. I wanted to go see the birds, horses or even the sheep. Instead, we followed her car into town and, once there, Mum said I could have a quick walk. She must have noticed how on edge I was by my jiggling leg. The rainy morning had completely cleared, and the sun shone down on the small town. I got an ice cream and sat at the beach. I needed to find a library – I needed so much more knowledge. The rugby playing Māori guy from the funeral walked past and lifted his eyes as a greeting to me. I smiled back at him. He and some others started throwing a ball around. As the ball headed in my direction, he ran over. 'Do you want to play?' he asked.

Seeing I had just had the last bite of my cone, I had no excuse not to.

I shrugged. 'Sure.'

He threw the ball at me, and I started running.

I'd always been competitive – I was sure all the locals knew that after the first minute of me joining in.

'Score!' I screamed as I got my first try. 'In your face.'

The locals laughed at me, including me in every part of the game. By my third try, I was covered in mud and had almost forgotten about my responsibilities and concerns back at the farm. They all came crashing back to me as the cute local accidentally crashed into me, twisting my ankle. And then he sprinted off. I'd been one of the locals running around. But now I was on the ground, hugging my throbbing ankle.

'Sore loser,' a girl spat, walking away.

Tears ran down my face, and I started shaking and sobbing. The others walked off muttering words like 'crybaby,' I wanted to call behind them that I had been winning. But I wasn't strong enough. The cute guy who asked me to play came back with ice in a paper towel from the ice-cream truck.

'Sorry,' I sobbed.

'I'm the one who's sorry,' he said.

'It's not the ankle.'

'What's not the ankle?' he asked, lifting the ice and putting it on my purple bump.

'Owwww!'

I reached out and put my hand on his, moving the ice back to the lump.

'The tears – I have a lot on my plate – I need to be able to feed my animals.'

'I heard. Can I help?'

'Do you know of any large, colourful native frogs?'

'No, even introduced frogs are greens and browns,' he spoke with such conviction.

'So, if I said I had a bright orange frog?'

'The poison dart frog is orange - that's the only one that comes to mind. And if you have one of them, you have trouble,' he said.

I already knew I had trouble.

Mum's voice broke into our conversation. 'Bee, where are you?'

'Oh bugger, I forgot my phone again.' I told him.

'I thought girl's phones were attached to them.'

'You see, I'm not a typical teen,' I told him.

'I see that,' He laughed, helping me up as I hopped towards my flustered Mum.

'What on earth?' Mum ran towards us.

'I'm okay, Mum.'

'Not from where I'm standing – let's go.'

Hours at A and E, x-rays and doctor's questions all ate into my animal time. I wanted to go home, but not with the moonboot and bagful of medicine that I arrived with.

I spent most of the next day at the table going through accounts. Resting my leg and taking painkillers, the only animals I saw were Marmalade and Basil. My Aunty had taken her family out to the beach for the morning. Mum cleared the table of paperwork for lunch. I sat back and saw I had drawn frogs, snakes, hedgehogs, and possums. I'd been drawing them on my pad where numbers should have been. 'Sorry,' I said, looking up at Mum.

She laughed. 'Can't take the animals out of you, love.'

Chapter 10: Truck

Belinda

Aunty made dinner, and it smelt homely, which was great as the atmosphere wasn't. The horrid silence at the dinner table was only broken by scraping cutlery. The four farm employees didn't join us this time. The sun was still shining, but it was chilly. I guessed if I got up to get a hoodie I would be told to stay seated, so instead I ate as quickly as I could without choking.

After five minutes of awkwardness, Lily said, 'Wasn't the weather nice today?'

'Really? We are talking about the weather?' Aunty Carol muttered.

Finally, Sofie said, 'How rich are you, Belinda?'

Everyone's cutlery stilled, and they turned to wait for me to answer. Aunty Carol shushed Sofie but glared at me with the others.

'It's all too weird talking about it,' I mumbled.

Not long after starting the dishes, Aunty Carol sent me out of the kitchen, so I hopped out towards the aviary. They didn't even want me near them. I wanted this farm, but I would give it up for my family to still love me.

On my way to my feathered family, the family that still loved me, from the corner of my eye I glimpsed movement. It was Jason carrying a box to Murray's truck. When he walked away, I snuck into the back of the truck to see what it was. The noises in there were horrid.

Screeches and hisses, and an almighty bang. The noise of the truck door rolling down as the enclosed truck bed got darker and darker. Too dark to see my hand in front of me, which I slid into my pocket, it was empty. Why hadn't I grabbed my phone? I never had it when I needed it. No one would even notice I was gone. Mum may – no I was becoming too independent. I turned around to face the front of the truck.

The engine started up, and we rumbled down the driveway. I counted the left and right turns. Each turn I had to hold myself so I didn't fall and crash. I remember being shut in a closet when I was younger, it was horrible, this is bigger but just as dark and claustrophobic, and so much more dangerous, and cold. I really wish I had got my hoodie, I wanted to put something around my shoulders but with the scary noises in the dark with me I didn't want to poke around. Could the animals smell my fear? We couldn't have been on the road for more than ten minutes and only eight turns when the truck rumbled to a stop.

The door rolled up, daylight blinded me for a moment, and I quickly slid out of sight. Only two of them were there, Murray and Jason, and they offloaded twenty or so crates before closing the door. Not coming near the back where I was thankfully. I had peeked a few times when their voices had faded and saw a storage unit. There were no blankets for warmth either, just crates and boxes, I looked in a few near me and they were empty but the one that had just been offloaded had growled.

The storage unit was full of crates on one side and food and buckets of water on the other side. If I had my phone, I could've taken photos. Surely this proved they were up to something, or maybe it didn't, and they were delivering animals to pet shops. That was the state of the business, after all. I ducked as I heard Jason's voice. 'It was a great game. Any time we beat the Ozzies is a great game.'

'Ah, shut up,' Damion said. There was a twang in his voice I hadn't noticed before, but he was Australian.

The trip back was so quiet without the hoots and screeches. Once home, the truck turned off, and the voices quieted. They didn't open the back. At least they didn't know I was there. I waited and heard more voices, not close enough to make them out, then all human noises faded away. How late was it? How long would I be in here? I heard the front door open, and someone climbed in. ohhhh nooo, Would the truck drive away and I'd end up in Kaitaia all alone? Gisborne? Or Wellington? Had my family noticed I wasn't around yet?

The driver closed the door again and locked it. I should've escaped. After what seemed like years, I stood, shaking off the pins and needles, and hobbled toward the back door. I tripped and fell. The noise of my shoulder hitting the roller door was almost loud enough to wake Uncle Jerry.

I ducked down again and waited. My ankle throbbing more intensely than my pounding heart.

'What was that?' Murray called. They rolled the door up, as I hobbled out of sight, taking my moon boot off to rub my throbbing ankle. I heard them looking at the front of the truck and slid my jacket over my face. I could see Jason's shoe but after a brief pause it turned and walked away, 'Maybe it was some stupid bird or possum.'

I slid the bottom of the boot under the door as Jason rolled it down.

I waited a little longer before slowly pushing the door up half a meter. I crawled out and closed it behind me. Then hobbled as far away from the truck as I could to hide. Just in time too, as Murray came back. 'Jason, did you close the truck door?'

'I think so.'

'Did you lock it?'

'Not sure.'

'Dumb ass,' Murray locked the door, and the two of them carried on, looking around to see if anyone was watching.

I was watching. I put my boot back on and limped towards the house.

'Have you been with the birds or beasts?' Uncle Charlie asked me as I entered the house.

'Beasts,' I said. 'Mum, I need help with my ankle.'

Mum re-wrapped my ankle and gave me pain killers – along with a *rest your ankle* lecture. I winced from the pain, and was sad from the frustration, and from the secrets I wasn't ready to share.

'It's late, love. Bedtime.' Mum had a drink in hand, and the adults looked settled in for the night. With my ankle wrapped in a bread bag, I had a long shower with Marmalade. I felt dirty. Like those men, dirty. But were they all dirty? A shower with Marmalade was like therapy. It was one of our special times, just the two of us in the water. She loved to drink from the shower head and did a little dance thing with her feathers. After, I read myself to a dream world where Ruby and I were galloping around the farm.

Chapter 11: Caught!

Belinda

I woke up at three in the morning again. Why was this happening every night? I tried to fall asleep, but I couldn't get the birds out of my mind. Something was wrong, and it was clear I wasn't going to get any sleep until I got up to investigate. After taking fresh pain killers, Basil and I crept out. Men's gruff voices had me on alert. There was a big truck backed up to the shed that Nigel had warned me not to go into. For my safety! How naïve had I been? I had to get a closer look, but I was not going in the truck this time. Why was there a big truck at the farm in the early hours of the morning? This truck was much bigger than yesterday's truck.

Something was going down. The men were loading boxes in the back. My boxes? I'd learnt my lesson and had my phone with me, so I took it out and started recording, leaning it up against a tree. I suspected the crates were full of live animals, *my* animals. I made sure my phone captured photos of all four men carrying boxes. All four of them. Why Nigel? As I was putting my phone back in my pocket, I touched something by mistake, and my phone made a noise. Murray was the closest and he froze, looking at the bush I was in. He walked towards me and I stopped breathing. The closer he got, I realised that in his hand was a gun, a small one. It looked as legal as the Kiwi in the cages were. Oh my gosh, he was going to kill me. The bushes backed into a shed, nowhere to run, nowhere to hide. As still as I was, my heart was thumping so intensely, I bet the bush was shaking. I was going to die, just like Uncle Jerry had, even in the same place.

Just then Basil shuffled out from beside me, he weed on a bush in front of Murray and ran off towards the house. Murray lifted his gun and pointed at Basil. I slowly lifted my hands to my mouth to stop my screaming. Then Murray said 'Bang' and lowered the gun. Relief flowed that he hadn't shot Basil. Murray walked inside the shed, and I shuffled down between the bushes and the shed to get back inside the house.

I hobbled to find Mum, 'Mum, Mum, Wake up! Something is going on outside. I'm going to get a closer look.'

Rubbing her eyes, Mum took one look at my wet and puffy face. She woke up real quick.

'The men outside are loading animals up in a big truck that's not one of ours and Murray has a gun. He almost shot Basil. He almost shot me.'

Mum looked out the window before calling the police. She told them everything and promised she would lock us inside safely. I wasn't having a bar of that, so when Mum was looking out the window, I slunk off. It hurt me to do it, but I closed Basil inside, leaving him scratching on the glass door.

'I promise to let you out soon,' I whispered.

Cautiously I made my way around to the back of the yard, ducking between trees and vehicles. I was close enough to the action, so I set up camp in a bush.

'We only have two more hours,' Damion's words were clipped and urgent.

Nigel sniffed. 'Less than that mate, Belinda is an early riser.'

'Yeah, but she's injured.' Murray snickered like it was some kind of triumph.

I wanted to throw a stone at him, but I restrained myself. My stomach clenched as I tightened my insides to hold on to my last meal. Nigel was involved. I had really hoped he was a good guy and could stay.

'Interfering, little bitch,' Murray muttered. 'Just because she can bring a horse back from the brink doesn't mean she can run this place.'

Bastard.

He dropped a crate on his foot. 'Fuck!'

I squashed a laugh. Karma!

The boxes were in many sizes, and surprisingly quiet, so I didn't know what was in them. One crate was huge; Nigel and Jason both carried it. I saw Nigel give Jason's hand a quick squeeze. Maybe Nigel felt he had to help because he was threatened. The police slowly crept up the driveway in the shadows of the trees twenty minutes later, just like they did in the movies, looking heavily armed. I was shaking with fear, even though I knew they were the good guys. They came around both sides of the Manor and eventually got to the back of the sheds.

My staff were still loading the truck, but only three of them. Where was Murray? The men raised their hands in defeat when the police yelled, 'Police, stop what you are doing!'

Nigel, Jason and Damion raised their hands. They didn't even try to defend themselves. How could they – they'd been caught red handed. Nigel was literally holding a caged kea. I crept back to my phone and videoed safely from a distance as the three men were hand cuffed. An officer arrived with a police dog and the dog came straight to me.

'Freeze,' the dog handler said.

I stood up and raised my hands.

'That's my daughter!' Mum yelled, running to me.

Basil was running too, and he came straight to my side, hopefully forgiving me for leaving him behind. I couldn't risk him being shot.

'She is our boss; this is all on her,' Jason called out.

'No,' I screamed as Mum held me back.

'Her bird is illegal and needs to be put down,' Damion added.

'Noooo,' I cried. I thought they were nice.

Damion pointed and said, 'Well played, Belinda. We know where you live, don't forget us. We won't forget you.'

'Was that a threat?' I asked as the police officer put handcuffs on him and arrested three of my staff members. They were taken away and more police came to look over the property. But where was Murray? The dogs and police hunted everywhere, I told them he had just been there. Damion had left but his words hung around me like a bad smell. *Her bird is illegal and needs to be put down.* I could not lose my best friend even if she was a bird. What if Murray was going to steal her from me?

Chapter 12: Mission Marmalade

Belinda

I went inside and looked for a room to hide Marmalade in. So what if she was illegal? Would they put her down? No – I would fight for her – I would fight for all my animals, but she is so much more than just a pet. Uncle Jerry had used her to teach me all about raising birds – all the memories I had of the three of us, mixing up baby bird feed, having the food on a funny shaped spoon and Marmalade sneezing and the food going in Uncle Jerry's beard. Him teaching her to whistle *If you're happy and you know it,* and *The Addams Family* theme song. Everything on the farm is connected to Uncle Jerry – he had given me so much – but Marmalade was the best gift any girl without a dad could get – a constant companion when Mum worked late. And I would fight to keep her. I planned to sneak a cockatiel in from the aviary and carry him around for a few days. I would not lose my Marmalade.

Basil, Marmalade, and I explored room after room of the Manor. It didn't take long and we were still in the same wing of the house when I found a small office, which was only half the size of all the other rooms. The dimensions were out. Basil confirmed my suspicions when he started scratching at the bottom of a bookshelf.

'Too cliché,' I said to Basil before I started looking for hidden buttons. There were no windows, but I assumed the sun rose while I looked but couldn't find anything. Marmalade flew off my shoulder and went and sat on the top of a caramel leather lounger. Basil curled on the lounger as well. When I was exhausted from looking, I lifted Basil and sat down too, placing him on my lap. Marmalade walked onto my shoulder and started chewing on my hair. While I thought about what to do next, I patted Basil with one hand and absently ran my other hand over the upholstered buttons. As my fingers brushed over them, one seemed a little more prominent and I absently pushed down on it. Two things happened: the rug in front of me moved up a little, and Basil jumped off my lap and started circling the room excitedly.

I got down on my knees and lifted the rug. Beneath it was a trapdoor. I wrenched it upwards and as soon as it was open, Basil bounded down the concrete steps into the dark.

'What do you think?' I asked my bird.

'Let's go.' Marmalade flew off my shoulder around the room and back to my other shoulder. And we went down the steps. I ran my hand over all the surfaces until I found a light switch. I was not comfortable in cold dark places, but Basil seemed familiar with the place, which helped to ease my anxiety.

We walked a short distance along the passage and came up another set of steps into a room that was identical to the room we had just been in. Only it had a large window, a full bookshelf and a desk next to the window, which must have belonged to my uncle.

I opened the curtain and sat at my uncle's desk. I rummaged through the drawers and found files on all four of

the employees. There were bank accounts
and other evidence he'd collected over
the years. I quickly gathered them up and
transferred them to the duplicate desk next
door. I then ran to my room and grabbed
some bird food, water, and a bird stand.

After setting my feathered baby up in the
hidden office, I left Marmalade all alone and
closed the trapdoor, covering it again with
the rug. I hated leaving her in there, but
I used to leave her alone when I went to
school. She'd be fine. Hopefully, it would
only be for a short time. I went outside
where Mum was still talking to the police.
How was I going to get past them without
being seen?

'Go cause a commotion,' I said to Basil,
not knowing if he understood, but I pointed
to Mum and the police officers.

Basil ran to them and started barking.
As soon as their attention was diverted, I
quickly hobbled past them to the aviary. I
grabbed the most vibrant yellow cockatiel
in a small cage, which could fit inside a tote
bag. There were several tote bags hanging
up, and I had wondered what they were
for – today they were for bird smuggling. I

slipped my new bird into the bag and back out and sneaked through the trees. I looked around as I exited – not just for the police and other authorities but also for Murray.

Like a cat burglar, I made it inside to my room and into Marmalade's cage The cockatiel was cute – just young and instantly played with all the bird toys. I fed him a piece of celery and he got so excited. Then he walked on to my hand and climbed up to my shoulder. 'I think I will call you, Honey.'

The bird tweeted twice. Did that mean yes? I hadn't meant to have another pet – he was a substitute, but after ten minutes with this feathered baby I knew he would be staying in the Manor with Marmalade, Basil, Mum and me.

I wanted to feel safe and secure, but I couldn't do that while Murray was still out there or who knows where. I had seen him just as the police arrived and then they couldn't find him anywhere. How could he escape the police like that? How could he just disappear and be safe, he was the smelliest man I'd ever met. How could the police dogs not smell him?

I rejoined Mum and Basil on the porch. 'What's going on?' I handed over my phone with the video footage on it to a police officer. 'They were moving the illegal items from the shed to a lock-up they hired yesterday.'

'Really?' Mum had a shake in her voice – as if she only just realised we had been in danger. I hoped she wouldn't tell me I had to sell – I don't care what these horrible men did here this is my inheritance.

'I know.' I shivered, remembering how I had almost been caught in the truck.

'As in livestock?' Mum asked.

'Yes.'

'What kind of animals?' I asked.

'Illegal pets.' The man looked as if his job was to inform us – he sure got the short stick. He was missing all the action.

'Oh, like kiwis? I saw a kiwi yesterday but thought they were helping rescue it.' I had been too innocent and naïve.

'Do you think they were helping rescue the snakes as well?' a police officer asked me.

'Oh my gosh, snakes, seriously?'

'And scorpions. That's just the start. There are endangered animals, dangerous animals, it's devastating.'

'My uncle didn't know anything about it. I heard Murray saying something about how they were doing it under my uncle's eyes without him knowing, how they hoped they could do it behind my back, too.'

'You are a very smart young lady. He didn't let them get away with it. Jerry was feeding us information for months too, and well done to you for closing the deal.' The police told me. 'I am Sargent Smith, I will be lead on this case. Call me if you find anything out of sorts, please.' He handed us cards.

'Do you think that they harmed Uncle Jerry?'

'We are investigating that possibility.'

'Really – and we have been living on the same property as them?' Mum shuddered.

'For a few months we have been investigating this farm – have you not noticed the helicopters?'

'I have – it's the same as the city up here.' I thought back to the copter noise. And how Murray had told me it wasn't a police chopper and would be a farm survey or aerial photos etc. Bloody Murray, where was he?

'You missed it when I had a truck ride.' I told them all about my ride last night.

'Honestly Belinda!' Mum freaked out that I hadn't told her.

'We need you to find Murray then we will be safe.'

'We will keep a police presence here,'

'Thank you, we have space for you to set up an area at the other end of the Manor, Mum pointed at the house, we had enough room to convert the Manor into the police academy.

'I don't know how to look after the animals,' I blurted.

Sargent Smith said, 'There's a local vet. I'll get him to come over and he'll give you a hand.'

'Thank you so much.'

'What will happen to all the animals they were trying to take away?'

'Again, the vets will help us, euthanize the dangerous ones, Department of Conservation will help where relevant, the legal ones are all yours.'

'What if people have purchased them? What if they come and attack us because they haven't got the goods that they have paid for?'

'All good questions – we have a lot to sort out. If they have paid for illegal pets, they will get fined, or worse. You will be safe. We will talk to the guys and do what we can so that none of this falls on you. We one hundred percent believe that you and your uncle had nothing to do with this.'

'Nigel, the tall thin one, he didn't want anything to do with the illegal side of it,' I said to the police.

'He was caught red-handed, my dear,' Sargent Smith told me.

'I know, but he might be willing to help.'

'And Murray? He must be close.'

'The dogs are looking for him now. We will keep security close till they find him.'

We turned around and my family was awake and standing at the door, no doubt wondering what was going on.

The police officer said, 'I guess you've got a little bit of explaining to do to your family. We'll leave you to it. I'll come over and introduce Mark, the vet, when he arrives. Should be just after nine.'

As we walked away from them, the rest of my family shuffled over to Mum and me.

'You've owned this property one day. What on earth have you done?' Uncle Charlie teased me.

Mum and I filled them in on everything while we made breakfast.

Cindy was quiet. I think deep down she knew Damion was a bad boy. Even so, having your first boyfriend arrested for being a snake daddy was tragic.

Then I went out to see Ruby. Basil came with me, but he was distracted by the police, who were all around the stables looking under and in things. Ruby was standing there, keeping out of their way. So, I took her for a gallop. At least that got me off my sore ankle for a bit – though it was painful to climb on her I had help from the police officer that was trailing me. While I rode, he checked for Murray all around the stalls.

After my pony time, I limped toward the toxic shed; I'd never seen inside and wanted a closer look while the police were there. I remembered some of the boxes that were in the fridge and the freezer, so I told the police about them. By the time I got back up to the house, the vet, Mark, had arrived.

'I've heard so much about you. It is so nice to meet you, Belinda.'

I still found it weird that the guys who lived and worked with Uncle Jerry didn't know about me, but the rest of the town acted like I was a long-lost friend. 'Please call me Bee,' I smiled with my remaining strength.

Uncle Charlie had lots of questions for Mark and the police. He took the authoritative male lead. I had thought Mum would have, but she was heavily leaning on her sister for support. The twins asked the police if they could see some of the illegal animals. They were unsure, but they let them in the end. I tagged along just as curious. Cindy stayed beside her mum, literally clinging on to her arm, like she used to cling to her mum's leg when she was a toddler. I sent a smile her way but she didn't return it. Weird that she had broken down when it was me who'd been kidnapped and almost caught. When they get Murray, we won't be so scared.

As we were walking down towards the sheds, a van with reporters rocked up. We all turned and there was a video camera facing us. The news presenter was doing an article on us.

'Do they even know what we found?' I said quietly to Lily.

She was holding my hand in support. I had Basil at my feet, also in support.

'It is assumed they have found drugs, but we don't know which kind,' the presenter said on camera.

The police asked them to leave and told them there were no drugs found. A police officer was then placed at the front of the property to stop others from coming down this far. Lily was gutted cause she thought he was the cute one. I don't know how she had time to think people were cute while we were in the middle of a real-life police circus.

We were told we could see the animals, but we weren't allowed to video them or tell anybody what we had seen. It would need to be private for the court case. We were happy with that.

'I've never seen a snake before. I thought New Zealand was snake-free.' I looked at the closest cages. The birds I'd already seen, but the snake was something I'd never thought I would see in snake-free Aotearoa.

'So did we, young lady.' I think the officer's job was to keep us busy.

The snake was in a cage far too small for its coil. Poor thing. I leaned closer but it launched at me, hissing, and I was grateful for the bars. Bloody ugly thing can stay in the tiny cage.

I'd started shaking. In fact, I almost wet my pants.

'What if one of these had gotten out? What if it was my fault New Zealand had snakes everywhere? How would the kiwi survive then?'

That's when I saw kiwis, tuatara and keas.

'All these native animals would go down to Auckland to be looked after by the Auckland Zoo.'

'By whom?' I asked.

The police told us 'DOC and the zoo staff are on their way. The zoo staff will help the vet euthanize the dangerous and illegal animals. Museum staff are coming too.'

'Why the museum?' I asked.

'They store records of animals. Do you know they have a large collection of albino animals out the back rooms not on display?'

'Bee, have you seen paperwork anywhere, books with accounts or receipts in them? We want to find the records of who had purchased the animals in the past.'

Because of Murray and the misfits, people had purchased illegal pets, and they were in bedrooms and living rooms all over New Zealand. I shivered more knowing that kiwis may have been shipped over to different countries in the world.

'I can show you my Uncle Jerry's office.'

'Later,' he cupped his right hand over his earpiece. 'No bloody way.'

'What's happened now?' Mum pulled me in close as police from everywhere stopped what they were doing and ran down the driveway.

'Are you going too?' I asked him.

'No, I am staying.'

'Is there a new incident?' I asked.

'Murray.' He gulped. 'Well, he just stole my police car.'

My eyes were as wide as car lights. Maybe wider.

Mum walked off and got me a blanket. I was cold and in shock on so many levels about everything – Murray, the other men, the animals, the property.

'Are you sure you don't need to go too?'

'No, I'm here for you and the animals.' He stood straighter – focused. I bet he'd been trained to focus on traumatic situations. Having a kiwi kidnapper steal your police car can't be a good thing.

After an awkward silence I decided to ask Mark the most important question about my future – my animals' future. 'Excuse me, Mark. I'm really worried about the animals that are here legally. Nigel got up at three every morning and changed their water and fed them, talked to them, and replaced what they needed. I've been trying to watch what he does, but I need help to look after them, please. I don't know how to look after the bearded dragons, or the water dragons. The sheep, chickens, and the puppies. Can you help me find someone, please?'

Just then a young, tall, dark, and very handsome guy arrived in an old souped-up mini cooper.

I couldn't help but stare at him.

Chapter 13: Tamati

Belinda

The cute guy from the river rugby and the funeral was at my place when I was at my lowest, with a crocheted blanket I'd made when I was eleven around my shoulders. I needed a shower and was dressed like I'd been awake for three nights instead of just the one. Yet he looked crisp in jeans and a black singlet. He couldn't have been much older than me and wasn't as old as Damion, maybe twenty. He strutted over beside us.

Mark said, 'Perfect timing, this is my nephew Tamati. He's training to be a vet and has a bearded dragon as a pet. He's clued up with birds and stock.'

As he spoke, I looked at Tamati. He returned my glance.

'I think Tamati should take a couple of you into the reptile area. Once you have finished there, come and get me and I'll come down to the bird area with you.'

Tamati shook everyone's hand, leaving mine till last. He was confident with all the others, but as he shook my hand, he paused, with a look on his face that I couldn't read.

Did I smell? Of course, I did. He wouldn't know that I was the owner, would he?

I returned a confused look towards him.

The twins both came with Tamati and me. It was weird. Normally, Cindy came everywhere with me. What was with her? Was she still in shock and wanted to stay with her mum? Sick? I looked at her, but she was staring at the ground and moving dirt around with her feet. Part of me wished the twins had stayed behind too, so I could be alone with Tamati.

'Mum, show the remaining police Uncle Jerry's office.' Aunty, Uncle, Cindy, and Mum all went back inside with two officers. Hopefully, they didn't find the secret office and my Marmalade. I wanted to go with them - to run interference, but for now I had to stay with the other animals.

Mum had planned to get Uncle Jerry's clothes and personal effects and give them to the Salvation Army today. I wondered if the police would let her do that.

First, we started with the reptiles. Tamati's eyes were as wide as a cereal bowl. 'I've never seen such a large area with unique dragons.' His head turned, eyes bulged more 'never so many, so different, so beautiful.'

Blowfly larvae, mealworms, crickets, locusts. It was exciting and disgusting at the same time.

It took the four of us an hour and a half to go through and feed them all.

'Look at this, guys,' he pointed at a many legged- moving bug that he then picked up and fed to a lizard.

'Gross,' Sofie said.

I laughed, and Tamati gave me that same look that I didn't understand.

As he looked through the shed, he found a couple of lizards that were not meant to be in New Zealand.

Also, there were skinks, lizards and frogs that needed to go to the zoo as they were endangered.

'This guy's friendly. Anyone want a pat?' Tamati asked us, reaching out with a bearded dragon.

'Solid Pass,' Lily scrunched up her nose with disgust. Sofie did too.

'I would love to,' I said.

Tamati walked the reptile over and handed him to me. For a minute, the dragon was between Tamati's and my hands. I felt him move his thumb next to mine. That was one of those moments when I wanted to freeze time, yet my face was burning.

One twin pointed my face out to the other one, and they silently laughed.

I hoped Tamati didn't notice. He went back to feeding the lizards. The reptile climbed up my arm and settled over my chest. I instantly felt calmer. As I ran my hand down his spiky back he closed his eyes like he was loving this as much as I was.

I followed Tamati, watching him and patting my new friend. Noticing how he cared for them, but instead I found myself looking at his arms, were they warm like his hands had been? Then his chin. He had a strong jawline hidden under a few days' growth of facial hair. I had to learn to care for all these animals. Not check out the cute vet. I didn't have time for that, plus I still had a boyfriend, didn't I? No, I didn't. But I had to tell Brandon we were over. I took a big breath in and exhaled.

'Bloody big sigh that was,' Lily snickered.

'How am I going to do this?' I asked them.

'No idea. I couldn't even touch one of them, let alone care for it,' Sofie said.

'Belinda, are you the daughter of the new owner?' Tamati asked me.

I paused, thinking about how to answer this without giving too much away.

'First, please call me Bee. Belinda is an old person's name,' I started.

He stopped what he was doing and looked at me. I swear his eyes were laughing.

I ignored his reaction.

'Mum and I are staying here. She is going to do the management and produce side of things, and I'm caring for the animals, or going to give it my best. It's all so new, exciting, but scary.'

'I bet! I am happy to help if I get to visit these cuties.' As he said that, he stared directly into my eyes, and my cheeks burnt again.

'I will appreciate any help I can get. Thanks.'

Thankfully, some zoo staff arrived, interrupting us. However, the twins couldn't contain their laughter. Tamati showed everyone the different breeds. The zoo staff chatted with Tamati like a group of nerds at a comic convention. Tamati talked to them about the vet course he was doing and was name dropping his tutor.

I watched as they worked out which lizards I was allowed to keep. I tried to take note of what to do. Where to hold them, what to feed them. The twins topped up the water, so they were even helpful. By the time we had finished, more than half of the reptiles had been taken out by the zoo, for a safer or less happy future.

Looking at the reptiles didn't seem so daunting now, but I was glad that Tamati had promised to come back tomorrow to help me reorganise things and get a better grasp on the lizards. I was relying on Tamati's promise to help me. The twins got bored and left, and the zoo staff were loading half of the animals into their truck.

I said to Tamati once we were alone,

'My uncle was going to give me a lizard for my birthday, but I don't know which one was meant to be for me.'

'Let's observe these guys for a day or so and see which ones are the tamest,' he offered.

'Yes, can we?' I daydreamed about Tamati and me on a picnic blanket, eating fruit and having cute little lizards walking around us. I shook the image away. What was wrong with me? I was as bad as my cousins. In the middle of the most dramatic time of my life and I was having daydreams about some stranger. He could have a wife and kids for all I knew. A young wife – nah, no wedding ring.

We went back to get Mark and headed to the aviary to see what birds I still owned. He was with a group of people who I was told were our neighbours. Interestingly, the twins had reappeared now. Two of the neighbour's sons were around our age, with spiky blonde hair, blue eyes and wearing labelled clothes. The boys were looking at us too. I looked at Tamati. I much preferred the tall, dark and handsome type now. These blonde guys were like Brandon, not my type anymore. I needed to stop thinking about romance and focus again. I was still looking at Tamati. Oops, he had noticed too.

Mark introduced me to a man in short black stubbies and a red and black jumper, in other words, he looked like every farmer I'd ever seen on TV. The twins went to get Mum.

'These are the neighbours, they own 70% of the cows,' he said, pointing at the paddock.

'Oh, I heard you milk the cows every morning,' I said.

'Yes, we just wanted to introduce ourselves.'

'Hi, my name is Bee.' I went up and shook their hands.

By that stage, Mum had come down from the house and introduced herself as well. The twins rejoined us, but still no sign of Cindy.

I said, 'We don't know what the future is, but for now we would like to continue the deal that Uncle Jerry made with you.' I didn't want to commit to anything before Mum and I had a full understanding of the farm and animals.

They were happy when I told them.

'I love animals, but we only had four pets back home, and this is a lot more than four animals to look after.'

'If you need a hand, we're more than happy to help. Here's our number.' The man offered out a business card with a cow logo.

Mum reached out and took the card from him.

'Also, happy to take some chickens off your hands,' one of the boys laughed.

'Chickens?' Mum asked, her eyebrows creased. I had not seen chickens, but the fridge had been stocked with eggs by Murray every morning. Murray – I wondered where he was. Would he come back to hurt us? There was always a dangerous look in his eyes – like he could snap any moment and now he had snapped were the animals safe, my family safe? I shivered just thinking about him and his gross smell that lingered even after he'd left the room. I needed a distraction. 'Can we go see the chickens now then?'

Tamati said, 'Everyone's heard about the Loveridge's chickens.'

We walked with several police, away from the chaos, and across the paddocks.

'What's the smell?' Lily asked.

Was it smelly Murray?

'The chickens.' A neighbour replied.

'I hear we are close.' Mum added.

There was a tall hedge, and as we rounded it, we saw chickens everywhere. How could there still be places on this property I didn't know about?

'Holy,' Tamati said. 'I have been to chicken farms smaller than this!'

'Mrs. Loveridge, you have too many chickens in this area,' Mark laughed.

All the locals nodded.

Mum and I looked at each other, lost in their laughs.

'Why are you laughing?' I asked.

'You have enough chickens here to start an egg factory, so unless that's what you're planning to do, I highly recommend you sell some of them. They are going to be a lot of work, a lot more work than four pets are to look after,' Mark said. 'We would be more than happy to help if you need a hand.'

We agreed they would take twenty percent of the chickens each. Their grins showed how stoked they were.

I was excited too, as I made them an offer. 'Instead of paying for the chickens, can you please help a bit with fences and other jobs around the farm? Teach us a little about farm life.'

'Absolutely – I will too.' Mark and the neighbour agreed. Thankfully, they were keen to help me. I needed help.

Slowly, this huge, big land with lots of animals was becoming more manageable. We walked around the paddocks back towards the shed.

'Do you know anyone who wants a poodle breeding business? They aren't my thing.'

'Not my Hikarere?' Lily said.

'The white one?' Tamati grinned.

'Go on, show us.' Mark sounded excited as we walked into the poodle area.

'All yours.' The neighbours laughed, watching Mark's face.

'Please?' Mark asked, his face looked like mine used to on Christmas morning.

'Please take them.' I laughed. 'But I'm keen to breed the goats. Will you help?'

'No,' Lily pouted.

'Sure.' Mark said, still patting a something-doodle.

'Just not the white one,' I whispered to Mark as Lily climbed the barrier and Hikarere jumped up at her. Finally, we got to see the birds. Well, not all of us, Lily and one neighbour stayed behind with the puppies. The zoo had already come in and taken the native birds, and others. I was excited to see the birds I got to keep. Mark was extremely interested to see our birds. He had never been allowed in there, and had never seen such a selection. With some birds, he said I could make a fortune if I sold them.

'I'm not giving any more of these away.' I laughed at Mark's opened eyes.

'I'm more than happy with the dogs and chickens, thanks. I may lose my wife if I go home with anything else.'

We all laughed along with him.

'The birds all have healthy plumage – so they've been looked after well.'

'More pressure – if I don't look after them they will loose their feathers?' panic set in.

'I can tell you are going to look after them perfectly.' How did Mark know. But I didn't want to prove him wrong.

I didn't want to sell any of them, but I guess that's what pet shops did. Sold animals. Sadly, the crossbred birds still had an uncertain future. He didn't know if I could keep them or not. He would have to investigate that. I would hide Marmalade whenever the Auckland Zoo and other officials were around.

Thankfully, it was easy for me to look after the birds because I'd already spent time in there and seen the last two days of care and asked a lot of questions. Mark was also excited to see so many eggs.

Where they would go depended on what hatched out of them. The zoo was interested in the eggs too. Though they wanted to take them all, they didn't have room for the eggs, so they said they would visit often and help me with the eggs and take the protected ones as they hatched. My hatchery was more advanced than theirs.

'Something has woken me up at three o'clock every morning,' I said to Mark.

'Well, half the animals and the workers are gone now, so it will be interesting to see if you sleep tonight.' Mum said.

'I will come by early tomorrow morning to help if you like,' Tamati said. 'What time are you up?'

'Any time after three, just come to the aviary. I'll be in there.'

'Sounds good,' he said. 'See you tomorrow.' They all left, and I went to clean out the stables, blasting music so I didn't have to think.

It was afternoon teatime before I knew it. I dragged my sore leg up to the house, where it was obvious the others had been busy. All Uncle Jerry's clothes were piled in bags on the front porch and there were rubbish bags to the other side. But the art was still up, and throws, candles and cushions were all still there. I was happy about that.

'We just got rid of medicine and things like that, love,' Mum said, reading the concerned look on my face.

'I need to talk to you,' Sofie said, taking me by the hand and walking away from the others. 'What's with you and the Māori vet, boy?'

'Nothing,' I said, as I blushed.

'He likes you too,' she said.

We were interrupted by Uncle Charlie's whistle that meant we all had to head in for a family conference. The police were huddled in amongst the family around the big outside table where we had shared meals with Murray and the convicts.

'Is there an update on Murray?' I asked. If they have him, we can finally relax so I was eagerly waiting to hear an update.

'As you know Murray stole my car, he was chased north. We lay nails on one road, but he would turn down a side road. We wondered if he had someone else's radio. He avoided all of our road stops and,' He took a big breath before continuing 'he went around a curve and at the next straight had disappeared. We – well long story short, we found my car a while later. On fire at the bottom of a rocky gully. We can't get it out without special equipment which will take some time, but we assume Murray didn't make it.'

'Dead?' I put one hand on top of the other to try and stop them from shaking.

'What does that mean for your presence here?' Uncle Charlie asked.

'We will still be visiting as we investigate the other three, we would prefer you didn't tell anyone about Murray as we fear the other three will pin everything on Murray if they know he cannot defend himself.'

'But you won't be here much?' mum asked, her arm shaking too.

'You are safe now. We are only a call away – any concerns I will head straight here.

'In a new car?' Lily laughed.

'Lily!' everyone else said as I hid a laugh. I don't know how I could laugh at such an emotional time, but I did. I wanted to laugh all my worries and concerns away.

It was of course no laughing matter, Murray the smelly was dead. Something else I had to come to terms with – at least I didn't have to fear him anymore. The police left the family to it, slowly driving off in pairs.

'Hey, Bee,' Uncle Charlie broke the silence this time. 'Well, that's a big stress taken away, so we are going to head off soon. We'll come back this weekend. Is that all right?'

'All of you?' I asked, looking at Cindy, who'd not spoken to me all day.

'Yes, love, we have some business to do, but I promise we will come back up soon.'

My face dropped. I had coped with everything, but only because my family was there. I couldn't cope without them. I hadn't realised I was crying until the tears began dripping off my chin. I grabbed Cindy by the hand and dragged her away from the others.

'I'm sorry Cindy. I didn't know Damion would get arrested.'

'You did what was best. I'm just sad I fell for him.' She wiped away my tears.

'I trusted Nigel, and Nigel let me down, too.' I said, 'He had kiwi and keas in tiny cages. It breaks my heart.'

Cindy held my hand. 'We will be back soon,' she said, wiping away the tears that were still rolling down my face. 'Sorry I have been distant today. I needed some time. I promise to talk about everything on the weekend.'

'Cindy, we have to leave,' Uncle Charlie called out.

We walked back to the driveway, holding hands.

'We've chosen cars and taken them out of the garage,' the twins sing. 'Is that ok?'

They'd chosen new model cars. Interesting. Those cars would not have been my pick. Perfect really. I liked the fancy old ones.

'Of course.'

'We are sorry we got jealous,' Sofia said to me.

'It's ok.'

'It's not. Look at all the stress you are under. You have had to grow up overnight,' Lily added.

'It's not all on her,' Mum said.

'Yeah, well, there is a lot of care required for those animals,' Sofia said.

'We got bored feeding them just once. You have to spend half your time feeding them and more.'

Lily chimed in. 'Uncle Jerry was right; we could never have looked after them.'

'No one could believe what you did with the horse,' Cindy added, giving me a supportive grin.

'Please think of this as your holiday home,' I said. 'Next time, we will set up personal rooms for you all. You twins can get a room of your own, no sharesies.'

'Truly?' Sofie asked.

I nodded.

'Thanks,' Lily smiled.

'I'm serious. This is a family property. It's all of ours.'

'You are amazing,' Sofie said.

'We better go,' Uncle Charlie said.

'Please don't,' I cried more.

Cindy hugged me, but sadly, they got into their cars. I waited until Uncle Charlie had driven out of sight before flapping my hands and getting Lily to stop.

'What's wrong?' she said. winding her window down.

'Wait just a minute.'

I ran off and put Hikarere in a dog carrier, filled a bag with food and some chew toys and walked them out to Lily.

'Really?' Lily was jiggling up and down.

'It'll be harder for your Dad to say no when you are hours away from here with the puppy.' I laughed.

'You are the best.' She hugged me one last time. She started talking to Hikarere as she buckled the cage in the front seat and drove off chatting away, 'Who's the best dog in the world?'

'You are Basil,' I laughed, giving him a pat as the dust settled on the driveway.

Although I didn't have time alone with Cindy, she messaged me on and off for most of her drive home.

Chapter 14: Makeover

Belinda

The farm was quiet – well, human quiet. There was still plenty of tweeting, mooing and baaing and, yes, cluck cluck clucking.

Mum said, 'Let's go to town.'

I dreaded leaving the animals. They were all my babies. I was the only one looking after them now. They all relied on only me to survive. Especially the eggs that may be endangered species.

'Come on,' she said, 'I have called the local school about enrolling you. Let's see if we can make this work—if we can pack up and move here.'

'Really?' I asked. That got me moving.

'Yes, so let's make the place comfortable for us,' she said, 'with new beds and bedding for both of us and a few books to read. You know you are a millionaire now; you can afford it.'

'I am?' I asked.

'A few times over,' she told me.

We got two new beds, and they said they could deliver tonight at six. We couldn't believe it. I got a queen-sized bed all to myself!

The small-town service was amazing. Along with our bedding and books, I got an art set and some canvases. We also got a new computer (which we put on the business), and we went to the supermarket. Although most of our food would be grown and produced on my farm (my farm, that sounded unbelievable), we got bread, ice cream, chips, peanuts, chocolate, popcorn, and crackers. We didn't need fruit, veggies, and meat. We would probably never have to buy fruit, veggies, and meat again, but I can tell you this: I was looking forward to having ice cream in a cone for dessert tonight.

We didn't get home much before 6 p.m. from our little shopping spree. Mum had even bought us some farming clothes. She said everyone who lives on a farm needs a Swanndri. It's part of being a

New Zealand farmer - Mum got a blue one and I got a red one. Mine was scratchy, but warm. We got gumboots too. Most gumboots I had seen came in red or black, but there's something special about small-town shopping, Mum got gumboots with sunflowers all over them, I got polka dot gumboots and because I'm gonna be spending a lot of time outside, I got a second pair of gumboots. My second pair had daisies on them, like my best friend back home, so I had a little of the city with me on the farm. Thankfully, the swelling in my ankle had reduced but not enough, I would only be wearing one fancy boot and a moonboot for a while yet.

I texted a photo of me and my daisy gumboots to Daisy. She sent back a laughing emoji. When we got back to the Black Manor, I quickly bustled around to clear everything out of the way so that the old bed could be removed. It would be donated to a charity like a lot of Uncle Jerry's things had already been. The new beds came within the hour and we got all set up.

We'd bought a colourful rug and matching cushions for my space. The room still had the old curtains, and the beautiful old wooden desk covered in floral carvings. Mum surprised me with a lamp for the old desk. I was set up now. All I needed to do was to get some photos to put on my pinboard.

I set my art supplies up on my desk and put together the new shelves. My room was magnificent, but it was missing the most important things. I told Mum I was going shopping in the pet shop.

Although it's a hard job looking after the animals, it was going to be an extremely rewarding one. I could already feel myself falling in love with so many of the animals, especially the bearded dragons. I still didn't know which bearded dragon Uncle Jerry was going to give me for my birthday, but I knew that one of those cuties was going to be my last gift from him. I would treasure them all and treat them like the most special gift here until I worked out which one it was or chose one.

There was a pet shop at the front of the property, and I had spent no time in there. I

wanted to see if there was a dragon set-up.
When I entered the shop for the first time, I
was shocked. The shop was full of animals
too! It smelt horrific, so I walked to the front
door and let the fresh air in. I texted Mum
and Mark. Mark said he had forgotten about
the shop too, and he would help soon.
These poor animals had not been fed in at
least a day. I didn't know how to care for
all the animals, but I knew how to change
water, and clean up messes, so I set about
doing that.

But Mark didn't come, his nephew did.
The smile spread across my face when
I saw Tamati, he was grinning too. I'd
enjoyed my time with Tamati and the
reptiles a little too much earlier in the day.
The last time he was here, he had the
beginning of facial hair, but now his face
was smooth. I wanted to touch it. What's
wrong with me?

Together, we fed the animals, cleaned
cages. Each time he passed me, or we were
close, we subtly touched. I noticed he smelt
nice now, too. Was he trying to impress me?
Did I want to be impressed? I already was!

Brandon who?

Mum came into the pet shop, and she looked into the register and did the accounting that she could see needed to be done. The shop was only open some days and was staffed by students and the four men. The students all had keys. We left a note for them to call us if they came and told them what we had done. Mum went back to the house as she was still setting up her room.

'Want to help me set up a bearded dragon area in my room?' I asked Tamati, my face flushed pink. Then I realised how stupid that sounded. 'Sorry, I'm sure you have better things to do with your time. Thanks for all your help today,' I added.

He laughed. 'I would love to. In fact, can't think of anything else I'd rather do. Your family pet shop is amazing,' he fed a meal worm to a cockatiel. 'You have everything you need here.'

Together, we grabbed the best equipment.

'I guess I better ring it up on the till and leave an IOU or the stock will be out.' I had to start thinking like a businesswoman, regardless of my age – I owned all this. People and animals relied on me.

Then we put the gear in his cute mini and drove to the lizard shed.

'One of the guys said he knew which dragon was to be mine, but he's in jail now.'

We had a look at the dragons. There were about six that were a good age to be adopted out? We took those six out and sat down with them. I easily knew which one interacted better. He was more hand raised and climbed up my arm onto my chest. Like a weighted blanket he soothed me. 'Orange like marmalade I am going to call him Paprika.'

'Funny,' Tamati said feeding some capsicum or paprika as some call it to the dragons.

We put the others away and grabbed my new baby, putting him in the car, and we drove up to the house.

'Mum, Tamati is helping me with my birthday gift from Uncle Jerry.'

'Ok love,' she called back. 'Do you need a hand at all?'

'I'm all good!' I called.

'Okay,' she said as Tamati and I walked away from her, down the hall.

'Mum had told me no more pets,' I laughed as I opened the door to my new room.

'Wow, this room looks city,' Tamati said, looking all around.

'We got it all today, in a small country town,' I replied, standing up for myself.

'Ah, it's all new,' he said.

'Yip, you're the first person to see it.'

'I love it,' he said. 'You got style. Birds, lizard, and a dog, you got it all. Oh my, that bird is not normal. A crossbreed? Be careful who you show.'

That's why Nigel was so fascinated by it. We talked for ages after the enclosure was all set up, each with a parrot on our shoulders. The cage went on my desk, and I plugged in the heat lamp.

Tamati placed some large rocks as hiding areas and I added some food and water. A few times as we were putting things in the cage our hands brushed each other's, each time his warm hands heated up my face. I loved chatting to Tamati. We had so much in common. My room was homely. We sat and chatted about nothing. Tamati was lying on my bed. We'd put the dragon and birds away for the night, and Basil was laying between us. Basil liked Tamati, I did too.

The next thing I knew, it was six-thirty in the morning. We'd fallen asleep. Tamati had been in my room all night! My head was on his left arm and his other arm was flopped across me.

Chapter 15: Locals
Belinda

I froze, listening to Tamati's breathing. He was still asleep. I wanted to turn and look at him. I liked his dark hair, dark eyes, and chiseled face. Let's face it, I liked everything about him, especially his arms around me.

He felt me move when I tried to glance at him.

'Oh,' he said, waking up. 'Sorry, we must have fallen asleep.'

'Will your parents be worried?' I asked.

'No,' he said, 'I live in a self-contained flat at my uncle's, but you know what, we better tend to those animals. I'll need to set an alarm for tomorrow morning.'

Sadly, he then pulled his arm out from under me very smoothly and jumped up from the bed.

We had breakfast, left the house without waking Mum up, and went down to feed the animals. I took Marmalade on her leash with us, and Basil walked between Tamati and me.

After feeding and seeing all the animals, we started making the birds better homes by moving them into bigger cages or joining two cages together. Then the birds had even better spaces. We added branches from outside, and other enrichments. I even fed some of them mealworms. Every time we completed any area, I got excited, and Tamati laughed at me. I hoped he was laughing in a good way. I wanted to impress him, but I didn't know how. But as much as that's what I wanted, he didn't touch me or make a move, that's for sure. If he was going to make a move, surely sleeping in my bed, he would have.

At least a girl could dream. I caught myself daydreaming a little too much about him, even so we had a productive morning. Mid-morning, I ducked out to get some mealworms from the insect shed. The shed felt wrong. I could smell sweat and cigarettes. Murray? Not possible. Do ghosts smell? Weird, I decided not to say anything when I returned to the feathered area.

The birds that liked meal worms sung away as Tamati and I whistled and laughed together.

Mum called us in for lunch. 'How are the babies?' .

'They are all amazing. Mum, I love them all. How will I ever sell any?'

'Lots of them are breeding birds, so don't sell them all,' Tamati told me while we ate egg and tomato sandwiches.

'Cool,' I said with a smile. Oops, I was staring at him again. Thankfully I snapped out of it before Mum saw. But had he?

'How was your morning?' I asked Mum.

'The pet shop is open, so I went down and got a rundown on the business. They are doing online orders too, and we are having a staff meeting on Thursday at 6 p.m.'

'Sounds good.'

Mum then told us about how she had been in the garden.

'Have you been here all day, Tamati?' she asked.

'We both fell asleep, Mum. Sorry it wasn't planned.'

'You fell asleep? What do you mean?'

'Last night? We were talking and...' My voice trailed off. Mum was blinking at me then shooting a surprised look at Tamati. He squirmed a little but put on a bright smile. We were only sleeping, I swear.' After a long beat, Mum slumped back in her chair with a short laugh and shook her head. 'Right. Well... okay.' She looked between us. 'I think you both need to go and have a shower; lucky we've got a couple of bathrooms.' Mum jokingly covered her nose.

'That's okay Ms Loveridge, I'll head home and have a shower. I'm sure I've outstayed my welcome now.'

'Not at all,' I said, a little too eagerly. As he was walking away, he turned back 'Hey, Bee.'

'Yes.' I jumped out of my chair so fast I nearly knocked it over. He grinned at me while I'm sure I turned a neon shade of red.

'A couple of us locals are going to a movie tonight if you're interested. Have you been to the movies yet?'

'I didn't even know there was a movie theatre here.'

'Well, there kinda is. Is that all right with you, Ms. Loveridge? If so, I can come and pick Bee up just after dinner?' he asked.

'Please, Tamati, call me Tasha. Is there any chance you could come earlier say before dinner? I've just taken the meat out, and as always, it's far too much for just the two of us,' Mum asked.

'I'll see.' He laughed. 'No, just kidding. I'd absolutely love to dine with you fine ladies tonight,' he said with a smirk. 'Your cooking is much better than what I make in my flat. I'd been planning on baked beans. I'll see you at five, and Bee, maybe don't wear that.'

'Okay, see you at five,' I laughed with him. I tried to hide the mud and no doubt poo that I had everywhere. My clothes needed as much of a wash as the rest of me. He was in the same boat, so I knew he meant it jokingly.

'Mum, can we go into town? I want to get my driver's license,' I said. 'I'd also like to get something new to wear tonight to the movies.'

'Absolutely, I need to pop in and see Mrs McLaren, so that's perfect.'

While Mum was at Mrs McLaren's office, I walked around the town. I passed the local school. Was it worth transferring with one term left of school?

Mum said we would see how this week went before we made our minds up on anything.

I couldn't go back to my old school. No way. I couldn't leave my babies.

I didn't want to leave the animals for that long and a part of me didn't want to leave Tamati for that long either. I doubted Tamati thought of me as anything except a meal ticket, or a little girl.

And of course, there was the fact that I had a boyfriend back home, or did I? I text Brandon, *Still haven't heard from you. Looks like we are going to stay away longer. Send my love to everyone. Bee.*

It'd been a week, and he hadn't messaged me at all. How serious could we be? My mind was made up. I would tell him we were over as soon as I could.

Tamati left my place two hours ago, and he had already messaged me a few times to see how things were, and he even sent me a bearded-dragon meme.

He received a bird meme from me.

How long do you not hear from someone before you've stopped dating them?

I suppose if I didn't live in the same town as Brandon that made it easier, at least I wouldn't run into him at school. We'd been together for a year and a half, that's a long time even if we had been drifting apart for a while.

I texted a few messages to Daisy, but didn't tell her much, and she didn't mention Brandon.

As I walked around town, while Mum sorted business, I began to feel at home. I booked a driving test for a month away before returning to the clothing shop. The sales lady smiled at me. Back home, you had to go to ten stores to get an outfit, but this one little shop had everything I needed.

I was set for the movies after ten minutes, and it was the same shop I'd got my farming clothes from yesterday.

Yet, I still had time, so I went to get my hair cut. They even painted my nails for free while I waited.

This town was amazing, I hoped Mum loved it like I did. I left the hairdressers and bumped into Tamati.

'Fancy seeing you here,' he grinned.

'Hey, I just had my hair cut.' I ran my fingers through my auburn hair. It was shorter now, but still longer than most girls.

'Looks good. That's where I'm going. Great minds think alike.'

'This town's amazing,' I said to him. Lifting my hands up in the air and spinning around. 'I love your raw energy,' he grinned.

'What does that mean?' my eyebrows creased.

'I just enjoy being around you,' he said.

'I thought you were taking pity on me.' My lips tightened.

'If I was taking pity on you, I would kiss you on your forehead,' he said.

He leaned in to kiss my forehead and moved to my cheek instead.

'So, what does that mean?' I asked, feeling lightheaded.

'Means I'm a little closer to my goal,' he said with a wink. 'Gotta go. I've got a date tonight and need to look good.'

'You already do.' I winked at him. Oops, I was a flirt too. I was allowed to flirt. I planned to be single. Same thing, isn't it?

'Perfect,' he ran off into the hairdressers.

OMG, he did like me too. I wanted to do a dance there in the street, but I suspected he could still see me from the barbers chair. Mum was still with Mrs McLaren, so I walked around the shops, trying to avoid the hairdressers. Some other guys came over to talk to me.

'Well, well, well, who are you?' one said.

My skin prickled as a guy walked closer, looking down on me. The smoke I could smell on his breath made me want to cough, but I held it in.

'Oh, I know. Jerry's niece,' another added. I could smell alcohol on him.

'You're rich now. Can you give me some money?' another asked.

They started crowding around me. I was getting scared, but then I heard Tamati's voice.

'Get away from her.' Tamati came stomping over, nostrils flaring. Slowly, I slid behind Tamati, feeling secure. I felt like I was going to cry as soon as he was close to me.

Like he was going to pick me up and I would curl up in a ball and he would keep me safe and secure forever.

'What's it to do with you?' a guy said to Tamati.

'She's with me. Leave her,' he said his voice like steel.

'She is not. I am,' a girl said, who I couldn't see for a mass of faces.

'Not anymore Penny. Remember, we ended things. I meant it.' Tamati spat.

'Come on, Bee,' he said, putting his arm around me. And we walked away from them.

'You, ok?' He asked when we were far enough away.

Those tears I had tried to swallow had escaped. Oh, the shame!

'I thought it was lovely here, but I just realised I don't know anything about this place. Were they the local kids?'

'No! That's the local dickheads and half of them are my cousins, so they will treat you better from now on. Tonight, you will meet the sane kids your age,' he said, kissing me on the forehead.

'That's a pity kiss,' I spat.

'It sure is,' he winked.

He was still holding me.

To start with, it had been a *guiding me to safety* hold, but now it was like a, *you're with me* hold.

I wanted to be with him.

No, I wanted to be single, and he's too old to look at me like that.

I looked over at the guys from earlier and saw a girl I guessed to be Penny watching us. She didn't look much older than me. She like me was brunette, unlike me she was in a short, tight skirt. I was in jeans with my wayward hair tied off my face in a messy twist. She had makeup on. I didn't even have make up here. Not that I often used it. Brandon had given all my makeup to me. Rude, now that I thought about it.

'Will Penny be there tonight?' I asked him.

'Don't really know, or care. She's not nice, a little bit screwed up to tell you the truth. If she is there, stay clear.'

'Do you mind if I move that cheek kiss to the lips?' he asked.

Wait, what did he just ask me? He wanted to kiss me. I wanted to scream, *just do it* at the top of my lungs. But I am not that rash.

He looked at the group of guys. They were still watching us.

'Are you wanting to kiss me just to show off to them?' I asked, feeling deflated about our flirting.

'No,' he said, 'I want to kiss you because that's all I have wanted to do since I saw you yesterday bossing the police around. And because of how cute you look, bouncing around with the animals.' He laughed, wiping my last tear away.

'Really?' I said.

I could feel butterflies in my stomach, his hands were on my waist, and I could feel the heat from them warming my whole body.

He started moving closer to me, but before we kissed, Mum came out of Mrs McLaren's.

'Bee!' she called.

Tamati stepped away from me.

'Sorry, Ms. Loveridge, some locals were harassing Bee, but I have sorted it,' Tamati said quickly.

'Ooh, thank you, Tamati. What would we do without you? And please call me Tasha. Now we have to go. This lady has an important night to get ready for.'

'See you soon,' I said, walking away. 'Thanks.'

Well, that was almost my second, first kiss. Not that I wanted my first actual kiss with Tamati to be in a street full of onlookers, including his ex.

'Mum, can I please stop and get some makeup?'

Mum walked me to the chemist and helped me get some simple makeup and a perfume too. To mask the animal smell. I even got a three pack of lip gloss including my favourite – strawberry.

Chapter 16: Should we or not?

Belinda

It didn't take long to get ready when we were home. I had a quick shower again to get rid of loose hair from my haircut, then I put on my blue-black eyeliner and candyfloss lippy. Although as I said, I wasn't a makeup kinda girl. I put on my new jeans and boots with a loose pale blue button-up shirt. Killing time while I waited for Tamati to arrive, I sat in Uncle Jerry's chair playing with my four pets. When he did arrive, he had two beautiful bunches of flowers, one for Mum and one for me.

'Thanks,' I said, kissing him on the cheek.

'Your turn, I see,' he said, laughing.

As we ate tea, Mum drove the conversation, asking about local clubs she could join, how we could get to know people, and where the library was. She especially wanted to know where I could make friends.

We had nachos for tea, not very romantic.

'The place I'm taking Belinda, tonight is the best place to meet teens in town. The nice ones. It's a youth group run by a church, but don't worry, she won't come back preaching to you. The kids are from the local school, boarding schools, and home schoolers, so a big variety. It really is a great place to meet like-minded teens.'

'That sounds great,' both Mum and I said at the same time.

'We are having a movie night tonight. We have ten-pin bowling, all sorts of other activities. I love our bush walks and are planning a trip next holiday to Camp Te Ao Mārama.'

'I have always wanted to go there. Cindy went there last year, Mum.' I said, more excited than scared.

'I thought you would like it.' He went on. 'There's the odd weirdo in town. I got in with the wrong crowd when I arrived here earlier this year.'

'So, you are a newbie too?' I asked.

'Kinda, I'm from up north. But I've spent all my holidays hanging out here with my cousins. And I love it here. I have been staying with my uncle, but his daughter comes home from uni soon. I'm not sure where I'll stay after that, but I hope to hang around.'

'We have lots of spare rooms here if you need a place to crash,' Mum said.

He just about choked on his food, 'Oh, I'm sorry, I wasn't hinting.'

Mum looked at me. 'Sorry, we should have talked about it. But this house is far too big for just the two of us. I guess the other boarders are not coming back so we should look for new ones, and someone who can help with the animals is a bloody good idea.'

'I agree, you should move in. Can you look after the animals if we have to go back to Auckland?' I hoped my red face wasn't giving me away again.

'Sure can,' he said. 'I think it sounds great. I have some pets too. Can you look after them when I have my vet classes in Auckland?'

'Sure. When are you moving in?' I asked.

'Tomorrow?' Mum suggested.

'Sounds great,' Tamati agreed with a large grin.

'What will we do about the rooms with the men's gear in it?' I looked towards those rooms.

'I think we should box it up and get it into a storage shed tomorrow.' Mum added.

'Have a spring clean,' I said. My nose scrunched at the thought of how smelly their rooms would be.

'If I'm living here, I want to help around the place,' Tamati said, carrying dishes to the sink and rinsing them.

'Okay, but you don't pay board.' I followed and loaded them in the dishwasher.

'No, I will still pay.'

'No, not if you help.' I agreed with Mum.

We didn't need money. We needed help with the animals and some security. I already knew he offered that. To me, he also offered companionship. I'd get to spend more time with him, and that's what I wanted the most.

'Ok, thank you Ms Lov.... umm Tasha,' he said. 'We better go. Don't want to miss the beginning of the movie.'

'I will do the dishes, you two head off, have a great night and thanks for watching over Bee,' Mum said.

'Do you want to take one of the new cars?' I asked.

I had not told him about the cars, so I opened the garage. His eyebrows arched and he whistled.

'Yes please.'

For the next five minutes, he was like a fanboy at a final rugby game, running around and jumping. He chose a new model McLaren, a red two-seater sports car. As I handed him the keys, he said, 'Thank you!' then kissed me on the lips. His hands were not on me. There was no romantic gesture at all. Just one small soft peck, in and out like it was nothing. I had not expected the kiss to start, but I had not wanted it to stop so suddenly, either.

'Sorry,' he said, 'I got caught up in the moment.'

He pulled away from me and acted like the kiss hadn't happened at all. We got in the car and headed out with a big beep and skid, showing the car off to Mum. Tamati turned the music on as we headed to town. We didn't speak at all until he turned off the road and drove up a hill. Turning the music down, I asked, 'Is this where the movie is?'

'No, I need to talk to you first.'

The driveway twisted and turned, and it was very narrow.

'You won't scratch the car, will you?' I teased.

'I hope not,' he said. No humor in his voice.

Even though I had tried to lighten the atmosphere, he was very focused. He was about to tell me the kiss was a mistake, and he didn't like me. Shit! Then the bush cleared to show the most amazing view all over the town, the river, estuary, and the ocean out to the islands. He parked the car, and I wandered around looking at the beaches, bush and farmland in 360 degrees.

'Wow, I want to see it all!' I said, taking in the view.

Tamati headed to a picnic table 'Come sit, we need to talk.'

I sat on the top of a table and he stood a meter away from me.

'Okay,' I said apprehensively.

'Listen Belinda, you and I have been flirting since the day we met, and it's a small town where we will always run into each other. You need to meet people your own age. I'm sorry I kissed you. We're going to be living in the same house. I shouldn't have done that. We are going to be in each other's paths a lot. I just worry we can't do this.'

Called it. 'Do what?' I asked him innocently.

'This,' he said, stepping closer to me and putting his hands back on my waist.

'Just friends?' I questioned, looking up into his big brown eyes, and I fluttered my eyelids in case that helped.

'Friends. That's perfect,' he said, but he was still holding me. Still looking needingly at me. Bugger!

That's when he slipped his hands off me and shook my hand, as if we had just made a deal. But our hands stayed connected. I willed with all my power. *Please hold me again. Please put your hands back on me, please put your warm lips back on me. Please Tamati, please.*

'Maybe...' I paused and licked my lips. 'Tamati, maybe we just need to finish that kiss from earlier and get it out of our systems?' I suggested.

'Okay.' He pulled in towards me.

He hadn't needed much encouragement.

'Just this one,' he said before our lips connected. His hands on my hips and mine mirrored his.

'Agreed,' I tried to say, but his warm minty lips had taken away my will to talk. How had I lived without knowing kisses could be this magnetic? Before I knew it, we were lying on the picnic table. I was on top of him and could tell he wanted more by the movements of his hands all over my body. The kiss was electric and unlike anything I'd ever experienced before. I don't think either of us would have pulled away if another car driving to the lookout hadn't interrupted us.

I rolled off him and he stood up.

'Sorry,' he said, 'that was a terrible start. It's like you have an invisible power over me.'

Then, standing a meter away from each other, he pointed out the views. 'Hey,' a blonde girl with long straggly hair said, hopping out of the car and walking towards us.

'Hey,' Tamati replied, 'this is Belinda, Jerry Loveridge's niece. I'm showing her around and taking her to our youth group tonight.'

'Please call me Bee,' I added.

'Cool, nice to meet you,' the girl said, looking at us quizzically. 'I'm Jessica, or Jess, or Jessie. This is Wiremu.'

'Do you go to the local school?' I asked.

'Are you transferring?' She asked me.

'I'm not sure about my future at the moment, but maybe?'

'Yes, I'm in year twelve.'

'Me too.'

'Are you staying at school next year?' I asked her.

'Yes, you?'

'I'm not sure, maybe.'

Wiremu took a step next to Jess and put his arm around her. She brushed it off and stiffened, turning away from him. I hid a smile.

'How about you, Wiremu?'

'I'm year twelve too, but I go to boarding school.'

Wiremu was now looking at Tamati. As if he was trying to tell Tamati something. It was clear the boys knew each other well.

'Wiremu and I are from the same Iwi up north,' Tamati told me. 'We better go. I have some other things to show you and don't want to miss the movie.'

'We are heading to the movies too, so see you there.'

'Ok, see you soon.'

As we drove away, he said, 'Do you think they saw us kissing?'

'Nah, they were too busy looking at the car,' I laughed.

'See, you're already making friends. Jessica is a great chick to hang with. I didn't know those two were together though, small town drama.'

'So, what else did you want to show me?'

'Nothing, I just wanted to leave. Wiremu clearly wanted to have Jessica alone up there. We have twenty minutes, so I will show you the best spot at the beach.'

'I love the beach, but I'd rather stay for more than just a few minutes,' I said.

'I know,' he said. 'I'll bring you back for a picnic sometime,' He winked. 'Oh sorry, I must stop flirting with you. I just can't help it.'

'You know I don't mind,' I said, holding his hand.

'You don't know what you want yet. Come on, let's just go to the youth group. If I take you to the beach, I'll lose control again.'

Chapter 17: Youth group

Belinda

We found a car park and got out. He introduced me to a girl called Anahera.

'Whooaaa, check out Tamati's car!' A group of guys said, walking over. The group talked car talk as I looked around the area. They were all dressed in black jeans and hoodies. A few had girls clinging on them. A few times Tamati tried to introduce me but the car chat interrupted him. I didn't mind. They were a lot to take in. Ten minutes later, Jessica arrived. She came straight up to me and took me under her wing. Introducing me around a bit, as did Anahera. Both girls asked for my number, and we said we would catch up. They were the same year at the same school, and they didn't seem to hate each other, but there was tension. Bet there was a story somewhere there.

Wiremu arrived ten minutes after Jess. I guessed they were a secret. I would love to say all the locals were friendly, but there was one girl that was giving me the evils. The hairs on my arms stood up as if she was talking to her friend and laughing about me. How could she have already formed an opinion when she'd never even spoken to me, maybe she didn't like my clothes, I was dressed similarly to Jess and Anahera in blue jeans and a hoodie.

We were in a Scout Hall by the looks of it, but after almost an hour of people chatting and the guys throwing a ball around; we walked five minutes into town to the local movie theatre. There was a roped-off section reserved for us, so we all went in there and I ended up sitting between the two girls. Tamati was with a group of guys, including Jessica's boyfriend. Tamati kept glancing back at me and my tummy flipped every time he winked and grinned at me. I don't ever remember Brandon giving me a tingly feeling in my stomach, like Tamati did. Jess laughed when she saw Tamati pull a face at me and once he'd turned back to the front, she nudged me. I lifted my shoulder in denial – I hope she took it as denial. When the movie was over, I walked back with the girls.

'What's with Tamati?' Anahera said. 'He's watched you all night like he's your bodyguard.'

Jessica added, 'I just remembered — I heard you had the police up at your place. Is that true?'

'I'm not allowed to talk about it till the court case, but I would love to hear what you heard.' there was a dreaded twist in my stomach. I always felt like that when I thought about the men, especially Murray, I still felt as if his ghost was lingering on the farm. I could smell him in the lizard shed.

'Well, the new owners—that's your Mum I assume—well, they called the cops on the staff, and Laura over there, well, her boyfriend was arrested. She said they hadn't done whatever they had been accused of doing, it was your Uncle Jerry.'

'Is that why she has been giving me the evils all night?' I asked, glancing at the scary-looking red head and turning away before she caught my eye. 'Wait, who's her boyfriend? I spent a lot of time with the staff, and none of them had girlfriends.'

'Damion,' she said.

'No,' I said with wide eyes.

'Did you hook up with him?' she asked me.

'No, but someone did, and Damion was really into that girl.'

'Laura and Damion have been a couple for months. They are sleeping together and everything. Laura was planning wedding bells and babies.'

'Oh no,' I said.

Tamati walked over to us, 'Come on, I better get you back to your mother's. You gotta get up early cause the birds won't feed themselves.'

'Are you looking after the animals?' Jessica asked me.

'Yes, with help from Tamati. He is moving in to help around the place with the things Mum and I don't know about.'

'So, is he moving in as your boyfriend, or like a cousin?' Anahera laughed.

'A friend, Mum arranged it, and she asked him to help me find some friends, hence why I am here tonight.' I focused all my muscles, so I appeared to have a poker face – hopefully.

'Sure, it is.' Anahera laughed.

Jess winked. Did she see more at the rest stop, if so, I wanted to tell her all about it, I wanted a friend to offload all these feelings to. Tamati interrupted telling me it was time to go, smiling we trotted to the car.

'Bee!' Jessica ran up to me. 'Two more things. Thanks for not saying anything about Wiremu and me. He was Anahera's boyfriend until a month ago.'

'Oh, I figured something had gone down with you two. I think she suspects you like him.'

'Yeah, me too, but we're not ready to tell anyone. My ex is Wiremu's mate, too.'

'That's the problem with small towns,' Tamati laughed.

'I have only ever had one boyfriend, and the time we've spent here is the longest I have gone without hearing from him.'

'You have a boyfriend?' Tamati spat. His face was screwed up, and his eyes had never looked so angry.

'Yeah, back home,' I said. I hadn't thought about Tamati being hurt, just about throwing Jessica off the scent of Tamati and I. I'd explain to Tamati later.

'What happens if you move up here?' Jessica said.

Jess didn't pick up on the fact that Tamati was now pacing and kicking the gravel. Oops not sad, he was fuming; I would explain to him sooner rather than later.

'Not sure. Guess I will have to talk to him about it.' I didn't want to go into the details with these people I hardly knew. Jessica seemed nice, but Tamati was the one I wanted to talk to. The sooner I could get him alone and explain, the better.

Tamati interrupted, 'We have to go, Belinda!'

Jessica ignored him. 'We so have to get together. I want to hear all about it.'

'Ok, do you know where I live? Do you want to pop over tomorrow?'

'That would be great,' Jess said. 'Bye,' she called behind us.

I got in the car.

Tamati had started driving before I had even put my seat belt on. He had also turned the music up loud and drove faster than he had on the way there. He drove in a different direction, too. When we stopped, we were at a beach. Tamati jumped out, slamming the door as he stomped onto the sand.

'What do you mean, you have a boyfriend?' he yelled at me.

'What about Penny?' I snapped back at him.

'I broke up with her before I met you. I'm single.'

'You said we were just friends, and you never asked,' I yelled, reacting to his mood.

He was pacing so much his footprints were all blurred into one line.

'If you calm down, I will tell you,' I added.

'I have spent the last few days falling in love with you, and you led me on!' he was still yelling at me.

I quickly glanced around us. Thankfully, no one else was around listening to this. At least he had stopped pacing, but he had his arms folded in front of him and was tapping his foot.

'I led you on?' I yelled back at him. 'You kissed me, but then said you didn't want me. You said you didn't want anyone to think something was going on between us, and now they don't.'

'Darn straight,' he yelled.

'Look, I have a boyfriend. He used to ring me all the time, but I have not spoken to him since my uncle died. He has not once asked me how I am or offered to help me! He and I are over, but it's a good way for Jessica to think you are just helping me out.' I took a big breath and slowly exhaled. 'And you know what else!' I yelled and took a step closer to him. 'My soon to be ex has never kissed me the way you do, or made me feel the way you do, or yelled at me with the passion you did just now.'

'So, you are going to break up with him?' Tamati puffed, his hands on his hips.

'Yes, as soon as I can.' I said, taking a step closer to him and reaching out for his hands.

'Do you like my passion?' he said through gritted teeth, but he had calmed down a little.

'Yes, I like your passion,' I almost whispered. I slowly lifted my hand up to his face and stroked it just once.

Tamati smiled, 'Sorry,' he was calmer again, 'I was so jealous. I don't understand this hold you have over me.'

He hugged me.

'I was so jealous all night. All those boys your age were watching you, wanting to talk to you. I really should just let you go. Let you be with people your age.'

'I met them, sure, but I know who I will dream about tonight, and I'm looking at him now.'

He leaned down and kissed me again. Somehow, it was even more amazing than before. All his pent-up frustration was channeling into his kisses. Hard and forceful, not as tender as earlier, but still breath-taking. He kissed me again and again. His hands were wandering, but this time they were under my clothes. Twenty minutes later, I started to shiver.

'I better take you home,' he said. 'I think we should come up with a plan, because staying away from you won't work when we are living under the same roof.'

'I don't want you to stay away. I want you even closer,' I said, kissing him again.

Chapter 18: Exploring

Belinda

F ast forward an hour and I was back home, and alone, but I was floating on air. I was asleep before I knew it and I was looking forward to the next day and all the excitement it would bring. I woke abruptly at three am again, so naturally, I went to look at the birds. That's when I saw that the lights were on down the staff side of the Black Manor, and I could hear noises. Crap, here we go again. I sent Mum a quick text, asking her to get video evidence in case I needed it. I was scared Mum wouldn't wake up but thankfully she did. Mum scanned the yard and walked in the opposite direction from my hiding spot. I didn't think she had seen me. Then my phone bleeped a text from Mum: 'Where are you? M'

I was in a different hiding spot from last night. I could see the silhouette of the man and didn't think I had seen him before. Who was he? He walked close to the bush I was in, and as he passed, a strong tang of cigarette smoke tingled my nostrils. He must have been a heavy smoker. He tried to open the shed but couldn't and gave up quickly. If he really wanted to get in there, he could have kicked the door in easily enough. He glanced towards where Mum was and I freaked, but when I looked, she was hidden from sight, thankfully.

I guess I should have been scared, but I was just over it. I wanted a stress and drama free day, reading or painting with the animals. The police arrived silently at 3.40 a.m. By then, the lights were off. A police officer spied me in the bush and gave me a thumbs up. He must have been over the other night. They caught the man sneaking around back inside and arrested him. He had a car full of paperwork. It was the paperwork the police had looked for during the day. Later, the police told me it was the records of who had purchased from them. That man's name was on the list. The police set up a task force to recover the animals from the purchasers.

What a relief. But was it over, could we take over here in peace now, focus on the farm, animals and business or was this rollercoaster gearing up for more twists and turns? If so, I wanted to get off, or at the very least stop at the top for a break and moment to take in the glorious view. All the paperwork had been in a hidden office down the other end of the Manor, behind a hidden door, of all places. What other secrets did the Black Manor hold? The police left a guard with us until the morning. Thankfully, they had a contact who was a locksmith.

The police said they would enter with us tomorrow morning and gather up the men's personal effects and take them to a storage lock-up. Mum and I lay in her bed for an hour. Oddly, we didn't talk. I bet Mum was over the drama, too. I didn't dare ask her in case she was thinking we needed to sell the Manor. I would rather sit in silence than have her say that. We heard another scuffle outside. I got up and saw the police officer was questioning Tamati. He'd just arrived in his little car. I thought the supercar he drove last night suited him better. I wondered how he ended up with such an unusual car, his new mini cooper. I ran outside, still in my PJ's.

'Hi. This is the vet who comes to help me with the animals,' I call to the police. Tamati looked like a bag of emotions. His hands up in the air, guilt all over his face, I laughed and as the police officer apologised, Tamati let out a big breath and laughed too. He followed me back to the house and I put the jug on while he flopped in the chair.

'Who, what, where, and why, oh, why didn't you call me? I'm moving in today,' he demanded. 'But you can't wear those PJs around me. They are too adorable,' he teased as he leaned over to kiss me.

'I thought we were not doing this?' I said after the kiss ended, then I leaned back in and kissed him again.

'We aren't,' he said, 'well, hard not to in your cute baby animal pyjamas.' He chuckled before pouring himself a glass of water. 'So, what's the plan today?'

'I'm going to have a shower and get dressed! Then do a quick feed of the animals. My family is coming back today, so I want to buy beds for them, and you and the police are going to help us clear out the other men's gear.'

'I haven't even moved in yet, and you are already Ms Bossy pants! Sounds like a good plan, though.'

'Are you around all day?'

'I'm on call for my uncle this afternoon, but other than that, I'm around, my lady.' He did a mock bow.

'I would like to see how the shop works, too. It is open today. Do you have a bike?' I asked.

I was sitting next to him with my hand on his leg, teasing. He had his arm around me.

'No.'

'Oh, I wonder how easy it is to bike around here. There must be some fun things to bike to without having to go to town,' I said. I think I will get some bikes. Cindy and I are going to get our license's soon but even then, it will be good to have bikes.

'I would love to bike the country roads with you and have picnics, but you gotta break up with your boyfriend first,' he added. 'Oh, there is so much keeping us apart. All I want to do is have a picnic with you and be with you all day.' He leaned in and kissed me.

'Don't stop,' I said as he pulled away again.

'Living here is going to be hard. What if you start dating a guy from school, which, by the way, is what you should do,' he said, letting go of me and standing up.

'That's not what I want, though.' I said, standing up too. And Mum walked in. 'What don't you want, love?'

'I don't want to be scared in this house,' I said casually.

'No, I was thinking about that. The sooner the locksmith comes, the better. We should change the locks to the sheds, too.'

'Especially the one with...' all three of us said.

But then we all said something different.

I said, 'birds.'

Tamati said, 'reptiles.'

Mum said, 'cars.'

I left the two of them talking and went and had a shower with Marmalade, and I put on my farming clothes.

'I'm off to feed the birds,' I said as I walked past them, stealing Mum's toast.

'Wait up,' Tamati said, running behind me.

'If you are so insistent on us not being together, you should do the reptiles today, and I will do the birds.'

'Nah, I love watching your face light up when the birds show you their wings.'

'Thought you were trying not to think like that?' I asked. 'You are sending mixed messages.'

'Said the girl with the boyfriend.'

'Not for long. Mum is talking about going back next week to get our stuff. Will you be able to help here while we are gone?'

'For sure, but don't be too long. I will miss you' He leaned in and kissed me more.

Yet again, he was the one pulling away from the kiss.

'You make me so jealous, you know,' he said. 'I never got jealous before I met you.'

'Well,' I said, pushing him over and getting on top of him. 'There is only one person I dreamt about last night, and one person I want to be with. And he's under me right now.'

We stayed there like that, kissing for far too long. So much so that we had to race around doing our morning chores. I saw Mum over the other side of the farm, doing her morning jobs, gathering the eggs and veggies from the garden for the day's meals.

'When's the farmer's market?' I asked.

'Tomorrow. Oh, you need to get some stuff together. The town counts on the eggs and produce that comes from here.'

'I don't want money for it.'

'It's part of your business.'

'Before they got arrested, one guy said they split it five ways with what they got and that it paid for an overseas holiday each year.'

'Well, your cousins are up. Maybe we could have a system like that. I have never been overseas.'

'Me either,' I said.

'Where would you go?' I asked him.

'Fiji,' he said.

'Really, wow!'

'Why?'

'Because that's where I want to go.'

At the same time, we both said, 'Snorkeling.' We didn't have to finish what we were saying, we just laughed. At that moment, Mum appeared. 'Hi. What's so funny?'

We told her about the markets, and she was keen. I texted Cindy and they were excited too.

'Cindy's half an hour away,' I said to Mum after getting another text from Cindy. Mum joined us in helping feed the last of the lizards.

'This is gross,' Mum said, putting flies in a cage.

'But aren't they amazing?' Tamati and I said at the same time. 'Jinks!'

'You two are so alike,' Mum laughed. Then she looked at us weirdly. 'How's your boyfriend, Bee?' she said to me.

Tamati turned away and kept feeding the lizards.

'I have not heard from him at all. I texted him a few times, but no reply. We've been drifting away from each other all winter, hardly seen him, so I will officially end it when we go home if he doesn't before then.' I glanced at Tamati when Mum was feeding a lizard.

'Oh wait, can I call this home yet?' I asked Mum. Joy filled my insides.

'It's almost been a week,' Mum said, 'and I can't imagine living anywhere else. How cozy will it be when we get our stuff from home? I'm thinking we may take a day trip early in the week, but the police need us here for now.'

We started walking back to the house with all the animals sorted for now.

'I forgot to tell you, Mrs McLaren worked out what money is owed to the four men and has officially fired them and kicked them out of here.' And on cue, the police arrived to get the men's things. I dashed into the house and had a drink and toilet stop and put some cute inside clothes on before heading to the other end of the Manor. When only Tamati could see me, I teased him. I could tell he was worked up by it. He wanted me.

The part of the Manor where the four men on the staff had lived was remarkably tidy for having been occupied by four bachelors. The police had a pile of boxes. We put on gloves and started to fill them up. We'd only been working ten minutes when the rest of my family arrived. Mum and I ran up to them like we hadn't seen them for a month. Not just a few days. We ended up in a big family hug. I had Cindy on one side of me, and Aunty Carol on the other side. 'Can I please ask you all a big favour?' I whispered loud enough that they could hear, but no one else.

'Anything,' Lily replied for all of them.

'Please don't tell Tamati or anyone else from town that I am the owner. They all assume it's Mum, and I would like it to stay that way.'

'Sure,' they promised.

'Are you sure?' Mum asked me. 'Even Tamati?'

'Please,' I begged. 'Just for now.'

They let it go and got stuck into clearing out.

We introduced the police to my family. While we worked, we talked about movies, weather, but mainly the markets.

Everyone was excited about the next morning. We found dirty magazines, drugs, and bongs, but other than that, it was only normal guy stuff.

'Do you think any of this furniture is theirs? Regardless, I don't want it.' I spoke.

The rest of us continued while our mums went and got more cleaning gear. We cleaned that end of the Manor like we'd cleaned the first side.

'Will you get boarders in?' Uncle Charlie asked. 'Or is this side just ours?' he joked.

'Yeah, we want to come up at least once a month for the markets. I will make bath bombs for the next one using that lavender outside,' Lily said.

'We already have a boarder coming in to live. Tamati is coming to board for free, but he will help us around the place,' Mum told them.

'Where were you thinking of staying, Tamati?' Lily asked.

'I'm not sure,' he said. 'I haven't looked around.'

'None of us have. Let's go from room to room.'

'It would be great if, as a family, you all had one area. There are six rooms, a lounge, and a kitchen here, so it makes sense for you to have this wing. If you agree, you should choose a room. We are going into town to get new furniture and bedding this afternoon, so find a room, get the measurements and you can choose your very own new bedroom.'

'In our own room?' Sofie said.

'Yes!' I grinned. 'I already told you that.'

'This bedroom has room for a couch,' Cindy said. 'Bags it!'

'They all do,' Uncle Charlie called out from another room.

We continued touring the Manor and found there was a middle area, like a lobby that all the rooms led to. We would make that room a big chill-out area and get some couches, bean bags, books, and board games. I was excited. I could see it all in my mind. From that room, Mum's and my area was to the left and Cindy's family's was to the right, but another staircase led up to ...where? Why had we never gone up the stairs before? We all walked up as the stairs went creak, creak, creak.

Chapter 19: Best room in the house.

Belinda

Upstairs was a wall to wall library full of animal and farming books, and a huge main bedroom with an ensuite larger than my lounge back home. The bed was a four-poster, larger than any bed I'd ever seen. It was phenomenal. We would get new bedding for that, too. Uncle measured the bed for a new mattress. I was mesmerised by the views out of the window that went in every direction. Bush, farm and in the far distance, I could see the ocean.

'Wow!' I said, walking around, touching the walls and windows, and looking at the views.

'This is your room,' Mum said.

'I have my room downstairs,' I said.

'Well, this is your future room.' She smiled at me.

I already knew I would spend a lot of time up there. The library was full of animal books. As the others walked down the stairs again, creaking as they stepped, Tamati came close to me and winked.

I went to kiss him, but at the last minute turned to peck his nose instead.

'You are so beautiful,' he whispered. 'You are driving me crazy, teasing me the way you are.'

'We still need to find a place for you to call your own space Tamati.'

Tamati pushed me against the wall and lifted my hands up above my head and kissed me. Our first kiss had been a bit of a fizzer, but since then, every kiss had been so passionate, and somehow the intensity was still heating up.

Slowly, he moved his mouth away from mine and started kissing down my throat and to the top of my cleavage.

'Oh, I want you too much,' he said, taking a big breath and stepping away from me.

'I want you too,' I said, following his step to get close to him again.

He lifted me up and spun me around, and as he put me down, something out the window caught my eye. I grabbed his hand and pulled him for a closer look.

'I just saw...' I paused and walked closer for a better look.

It was a small wooden cabin surrounded by trees and vines in a cute courtyard between the walls of the manor.

'There is a cabin out there. I wonder how we can get to it,' he said confirming he saw it too amongst the overgrown shrubs and weeds.

'I feel like I'm in a thriller,' I said to him.

'I will protect you, at all costs,' he laughed as he scooped me up and twisted me around, so I was on his back. He piggybacked me to the top of the stairs.

'Put me down now,' I said in a tone that clearly told him I meant it.

He relaxed his hold on me, and I slid down his back. None of the others were around. We could hear them in the distance, so I grabbed his hand and pulled him away from the top of the stairs for a minute.

'This may come as a small shock, Tamati,' I whispered.

'What?' he asked, intrigued.

'I really like you. My face blushed.

He started kissing me again.

'Are you two up there?' Mum's voice drifted up the stairs.

Tamati and I shared a last glance before I ran down the stairs. He followed behind me.

'Mum, we just saw a cabin out the window,' I called as I ran down the stairs.

'Charlie,' Mum called out, and we all went outside to look for the cabin.

We found a door that led to a private courtyard outside, and in the middle of it was a tiny rustic cabin. There were weeds covering a lot of it, so it's no surprise we hadn't seen it before. It was locked and looked self-contained.

'This looks like a perfect place for me to live,' Tamati said, looking at it.

I looked back up at the master room we had just been in. I thought that was the perfect place for Tamati to live. But I wanted to live with him. I was getting carried away again. After that, everyone started cleaning their rooms while Tamati and I went up to the master room again. We gave it a quick clean, and he said, 'The things I want to do to you in here.' He kissed me again.

I laughed. 'I think we get too excited up here.'

'I get excited anywhere you are.' Tamati lifted me up against a wall again as I put my hands around his back then I wrapped my legs around him.

'Fuck Bee, what are you doing to me?' he said, slipping his tongue inside my mouth.

A quiet cough broke through our passion. Cindy stood in the doorway. I slid down the wall and Tamati took a step away from me.

'It's not what it looks like,' I said innocently.

'It looks like he was about to take your virginity in a dirty, dusty old room,' Cindy said.

'You're a virgin?' Tamati asked, taking another step away from me.

'Tamati is a great friend who is helping me out,' I reached out for him.

Tamati took yet another step away. I ran up to him. 'But behind closed doors, he ignites feelings in me I can't contain, and quite frankly, I don't want to.'

'You're a virgin?' he repeated.

'So what?' I spat at him.

'Is this what you have been doing for the past two days?' Cindy asked.

'Kissing and fighting,' I said.

'We don't fight!' Tamati spat.

'See,' I said, raising my eyebrows.

They both laughed, and Tamati stepped closer to me wrapping his arms around my waist and resting his chin on my head.

'The police are back and said the bedding belonged to the men, so we have packed everything up for them,' she told us, never taking her eyes off me for a minute. 'The police are helping us move the old mattresses outside and they are on their way up here to get this mattress,' she added.

As she said that, the sound of footsteps approaching came up the stairs, and quick as anything Tamati was at the other side of the room dusting the window ledges. After the others entered the bedroom, Tamati made his way out. 'See you tonight. I'm off to work.' He waved.

'That boy is like an angel,' Mum said. 'He has been so helpful showing us the ropes. He has told me all about the area and is such a pleasure to have around.'

Cindy turned away from the others, hiding her laughter. I squeezed my lips together, so Cindy's laughter didn't become contagious. A group of us carried the mattresses outside and the last of the stuff into a truck. A skip bin had arrived, so we started filling that. Cindy pulled me away from the others and we went for a walk. I wanted to explain what she had seen.

'What on earth, what about your... like... boyfriend? where did all the passion come from?' she asked quickly, like she was in a hurry. I told her almost everything about the movies last night, how Tamati and I were not a couple but couldn't stay away from each other, and how I was going home to break up with Brandon.

'Have you been on the internet at all?' she asked me as we walked in the lavender field.

'No, haven't got it here. We talked about getting it but haven't missed it at all. Too many other things to do up here.'

'Well, Brandon has shared post after post about missing you!' she said.

'Oh,' I said, my heart sank. 'I have hardly seen him all winter.'

'That's what he posted, that after a crazy winter playing hockey, he couldn't wait to spend time with the love of his life.'

'Oh, shit.' My stomach did a flip but nothing like it had been, this time with dread.

'Yip!'

'I have never been drawn to Brandon the way I am to Tamati. I can see myself living here in that room up there with him, having his children.' I pointed up to the dome master bedroom. 'I see our entire future mapped out. When I was with Brandon, well, officially I still am, but there was never talk about our future.' Something caught my eye; I looked over at a shed and thought I'd seen a man there looking at us. When I turned back nothing was there, except a small puff of smoke which I watched dissolve in the air.

'I have something to tell you,' she said in her serious voice. 'About why I was weird before we left.' Cindy started shuffling.

'Oh, about Damion?'

'Yeah.'

'Well, I lost my virginity to him.'

'You what?' I don't know what opened up more, my eyes or mouth,

'Yeah!'

'Oh, my, I thought you were waiting for marriage?'

'Yeah, me too, but I got swept away,' Cindy said. 'Anyway, the first time was amazing, down in the trees. But it hurt Bee, it really hurt. I thought the second time would be better. But the second time it was in one of the sheds and it was horrible, he was rough, and I hated it. He even pulled some of my hair out and left these huge marks.' We both started to cry as I looked at the bruises on her arms. I couldn't believe I hadn't noticed them before; I'd been too caught up in my world. My heart was breaking for her, all the bad things those men did, Damion also broke my best friend's heart. I was glad he was in prison.

'Oh Jacinda,' I said, supporting her finally. 'You deserve so much better than him.'

'I know now. But when you had him arrested, I was so confused and angry at you. I didn't know it was him down there.'

'Sorry, Cindy, I do know he's an evil man,' I said. 'I have something else bad that I know about him. Do you want to know?'

'I saw his room earlier. It had disturbing porno in it. Rape and such.'

I didn't know whether to tell her about the bitchy girlfriend, I didn't want to break her, but maybe best to tell her everything now. 'Sorry Cindy, I have other stuff to tell you, but only if you want.'

'Yes, please tell me.' She nodded.

'Well, sorry, but he has a girlfriend. I met her last night.'

I told her that part about youth group, as I had left it out earlier.

'I should have said I didn't want to know. I don't want to talk about him and or think about him. I just want to move on.'

'Move on? You want someone else already?'

'I hate being alone. That's why I wanted Damion so bad. That's why I overlooked the red lights and warning signs.'

'You are going to find someone, Cindy. Someone who treats you the way you deserve. I love you. Come on, let's sort out that room of yours, so when you meet a nice guy our age, you have somewhere to make out with him.' I reached out to wipe her tears away, before wiping mine too.

'I like the sound of that.'

Cindy had another cry. I wanted to distract her, so we went into her room to clean. She didn't know how to decorate her room, but she seemed to love all my ideas. The adults chatted lots as they cleaned what would become their lounge and dining area. I overheard Aunty Carol say that she had quit her job and was going to follow her passion for painting. Uncle loved his job but had spoken to the boss and they were looking to form a partnership. Mum was in charge of the money I had inherited, and I was glad she offered him money to set up the business partnership. Uncle Charlie said, 'No, you have already given us so much.'

But Mum said, 'I've already got your account number, so what are you going to do?'

'You better take the money, Uncle Charlie!' I yelled out.

'Eavesdropper,' he called back with a smile in his voice.

We all had morning tea and headed into town. Being a Saturday, we didn't know when the shops would shut. Starting in the bed shop, we bought everyone, including Tamati, a new mattress. In fact, most of them got new bed bases too. Just a few had beautiful wooden beds like upstairs that we wanted to keep. The shop said they could deliver in three hours, so we also got linen, chairs, couches, desks, and lamps. As a surprise, Cindy and I wanted to set up an art room in one of the empty rooms on the south side. The art and craft shop had just shut when we got there, but they opened again for us and as we spent so much money, the lady said she would deliver to our place in a few hours.

We went and got some boring things too, like a vacuum cleaner and a new jug and toaster. Uncle Jerry's ones were just too old for Mum's liking. Charlie took my bankcard and went to the supermarket, so they had snacks at their end of the house. I was so glad I was sharing it all with them.

The twins came over to hug me. 'We're so glad you got left everything,' Sofie said.

'Imagine if the parents inherited this, they'd have sold it. We've never had our own rooms; this is so amazing!' Lily said.

Chapter 20: Bonfire

Belinda

Once we were back from town and we'd set up all the rooms, we got ready for the markets the following day. Aunty Carol and the twins made some things to sell while Mum, Cindy, and I picked fruit and veggies and put ribbons on them. Mum had been collecting eggs all week to sell at the markets, along with fruit and vegetables. She'd packed everything into crates and had it all out on the veranda ready to go. Uncle Charlie went to get some preserves, but I think he got distracted by looking around the shed and didn't come back for ages.

The locksmith arrived just before the rest of the deliveries, and he unlocked the sleepout as Tamati came into the courtyard with a box of belongings and a guitar.

The group of us gathered around as the locksmith opened the locked room. It had lock after lock after lock. Sargent Smith and friends joined us for the opening ceremony as they opened the door, the smell of cigarettes wafted out to the fresh country air I stood back, took a cough and the police officers told everybody under the age of 18 to go back inside the house, spoilsports. Turned out the horrible, horrible men had been manufacturing drugs. We girls wanted to look in the cabin but were ushered back inside the house by a policewoman and given more cleaning jobs. Wasn't fair, seeing I owned the place, but I didn't have the strength to fight it. I would let them be the adults for awhile.

Tamati stayed with the adults, and we didn't see any of them for a while. I was cleaning the bathroom, and I had lots of time to ponder. Was something in the cabin responsible for waking me up? Was that what the noises I'd been hearing in the middle of the night were? Tamati could not move in there. It would have been the perfect space, but aside from the fact that it was a crime scene, he didn't want to now.

With the bathroom sparkling clean and the police gone Tamati came and found me, and we moved him into a room in the middle of my wing. Tamati and I changed the furniture around and set up his room.

'How did you know what kind of bed I'd like?' he asked me.

'You said you liked mine, so I got the same.'

'It's perfect,' he said, pushing me on his freshly made bed.

'Hey, we just made this.' I pushed him away and got up and headed for the door.

We went to the bedroom across from his room, took out the single bed in there, moving it next door to make a twin room. Then we moved a couch from the central lounge to the empty room so he had his own space.

'Weird, two days ago I was helping you set up your room and now we are setting up mine down the hall,' he said to me with a quick kiss. 'I have missed you today. I'm used to having you to myself.'

'If this is us not dating, what's it going to be like when we are dating?' I asked in a teasing manner.

He pulled me back into his bedroom, picked me up and threw me back on his bed before jumping on top and kissing me.

'Oh well, I look forward to that then,' I said, poking my tongue out at him. This time, our kisses still had the same spark, but he had pulled his reactions back a little. He just held my hands. His hands didn't wander as they had before. I was about to ask if he had an issue with me being a virgin, and I guessed we were to have a fight about it when his phone rang. He was called out to help a pregnant cow, so he quickly kissed me farewell and drove off. That fight could wait till later. As I walked down to the kitchen, I heard knocking at the front door. It was Jessica. Bugger! I had forgotten to buy some bikes.

'Come in,' I said and gave her a tour of downstairs.

Jessica loved the Manor and got on well with all my cousins. The girls had set up their rooms, and they all had a list of things they wanted to bring from their home to personalise them.

We started talking about the markets and Jessica told us they always got pet supplies from our stall at the market. So, we walked to the pet shop at the front of the farm to see what we needed. Mum had spent time with the pet shop staff, but I hadn't yet. As we got there, it surprised me to see Wiremu working.

'I didn't know you worked here?' Jessica and I said at the same time, 'Jinks!'

'Yeah, I don't advertise it,' he said.

Wiremu introduced us to the other staff member, Dave, and I introduced my three cousins to them both.

'Has it been busy today?' I asked.

'Yes, just finished packing the stuff for the markets.'

'That's why we're here,' I told them.

'We've no idea what we are doing. We have eggs, veggies and preserves for the market, but Jess said we need to take pet supplies.'

'Absolutely. Do you know how many dragons and such you will upset if you don't take flies to the market?' Wiremu said. 'Speaking of which, we need more flies down here.'

'Damion used to pack them up every Friday and deliver new ones to us.'

'Oh gross,' Jessica said.

I nodded but agreed. 'I better do it soon.' I squirmed.

'We shut soon; I will help if you like?'

'That would be great,' I said, and Jessica smiled.

'Well, I have a bit of an ulterior motive. I have always wanted to see what's in those big sheds,' he said.

'Sure, I'll give you guys a tour. Maybe you could ask your parents if you can stay for tea. We always have lots of leftovers,' I said.

'Yes please,' Jess grinned.

'Sounds great,' Wiremu agreed.

'Tamati will be back soon. We have set him up in a few rooms as a live-in farm adviser.'

'Do you have any male friends who could come over?' Lily asked Wiremu.

Sofie was chatting up Dave, who looked to be our age, and was cleaning out a fish tank.

'Can you stay too, Dave?' Sofie asked.

'Sure.' He smiled.

Some customers came in and we backed away and observed the boys doing their magic. They were good and knew their stuff. I would have to spend more time with them learning about the business. I looked around at the shop. It was set up all wrong with stuff everywhere. Fish things were in different areas all over the shop, when it would be easier if they were all together.

'Imagine if the shop was laid out better?' I said to the girls.

'Do you have OCD? We could set it up in animal areas,' Jessica suggested.

'Ha ha, nah. They have an online store, too,' I told them.

'Yeah, I looked it up,' Cindy said. 'It could do with a facelift, like this shop.'

'The shop is open Saturdays, Tuesday's, Thursdays and Fridays. You should get a painter here on a Monday, Wednesday, or Sunday,' she said as we walked outside.

My heart skipped a beat knowing that Cindy had thought about this place while she'd been in the city, she was gonna help me.

'It's rustic out here,' I said, looking at the outside of the shop. It was made with exposed wood. 'It's like an old saloon. I should put in some hitching rails to tie horses to, and old wooden seats with maybe an old wagon, or at least wagon wheels, making the shop an old western destination.'

My phone beeped with a text from Uncle Charlie, wanting to know where we were.

I sent back, *At the shop, we have a handful of guys coming for tea, is that okay? And can you come help in the shop for a minute?*

A few minutes later, a motorbike roared up and stopped outside.

'Look what I found!' Uncle Charlie said, grinning from ear to ear. 'There are five farm bikes in total.'

We walked and talked Uncle through my ideas. He worked in construction and promised he'd order some wood and start building next weekend. Cindy had already found a rustic chair with wagon wheels hiding the legs for sale on the internet, and a few carts, so Uncle Charlie told us what to get. I was watching Basil run around and I started thinking about how I could build a small dog park in the front half of the paddock and get a coffee machine. I guessed I needed to slow my ideas down. I would throw my dog park idea at them once this area was finished. But I would tell

Tamati about it when we were alone next. The customers had left after spending a hundred and fifty dollars in the store, and the boys came outside with us.

'I would love to help,' Wiremu said to Charlie. 'I would like to work in construction after next year. When there are no customers, naturally.'

That sounded like a plan to me. Charlie and Wiremu got some measurements of the shop and outside courtyard and the rest of us shut the shop. Dave was showing Sofie a dragon for sale that he was patting, and he put it in her hand.

'Oh, he's cute.' Sofie said, patting it too.

Lily and I looked at each other and laughed, remembering a few days earlier when she thought they were gross. Grabbing the supplies for the market, we headed back to the Manor. During our tour of the house, we found Tamati in his room and he joined us for the rest of the tour.

'We should have a bonfire tonight,' Tamati suggested. 'We have piles of branches to burn off.'

In the bird aviary, Jess's eyes almost fell out of her head. I wonder if that's how I looked the first time I saw it. Tamati helped us into the lizard shed and sorted food out for the shop and markets.

'Can you guys smell smoke?' I asked.

'Dad used to sneak away and have smokes when he was stressed, maybe he's started again.' Lily told me fanning the doorway so the smoke drifted outside. As expected, Wiremu was buzzing out about the large shed and all the creatures inside, even the cockroaches. Dave was too, although he seemed rather distracted by my cousin. He was a fast mover and was already holding her hand. Jess and my cousins stayed clear of the bugs. By the time it was all sorted, a couple more of the local kids, including Anahera, had come out to join in our impromptu Manor-warming party. The large chatty group sat around the outside table back by the house and we ate barbecue. Mum had still made enough food. Many of the parents stayed and joined the party as they dropped their kids off. By the time the neighbours joined the parents, there were over ten adults drinking beer and chatting, and we teens slid away to a paddock. Tamati had a beer too. Would he hold me if he was a little drunk? The neighbour's children, Jack and Joe, went to boarding school, and they didn't know anyone there, even though they all lived in the same town for six years. That soon changed.

Another neighbour, Connor, and his younger sister, Elsa, came over. They were home schooled and didn't know the others yet either. Anahera took a liking to Jack instantly and didn't care when her ex-boyfriend, Wiremu, started holding Jess.

Connor and Lily went for a walk over to his place and came back holding hands. Elsa sat on Connor's lap but soon enough she warmed to Lily, as Connor clearly had, and Elsa climbed over to Lily's lap as Lily braided Elsa's hair.

We started the bonfire just after dinner. We didn't have any marshmallows sadly, but Uncle Charlie went out and found some sausages. After having had a big munch out dinner, I could hardly believe that we could eat sausages, but the fun of cooking them and how long it took to cook them on the bonfire meant by the time they were cooked, (or burnt as the case was for most of them) we had built up a second appetite. Everybody was socialising and talking to each other. Some people were walking off in pairs for parts of the night, including Wiremu and Tamati. Wiremu looked at me and laughed when he came back.

'What did you tell him?' I demanded from Tamati next time I could get him alone.

'Nothing for you to worry your pretty little head over,' he said, walking off.

Next time I saw Tamati, he was on the phone on a video chat. 'Say hi to my best mate Aidan,' he said to Dave, Sofie, Wiremu, Jess and me.

We all waved to someone on a video call, and he walked off showing his mate the birds. I had more friends here, and so did my cousins. I even saw Cindy chatting to Joe, and Joe flirted back with her, so I walked over to join them. Cindy was talking about the birds. Looks like my love of them was rubbing off on her.

'You should show Joe the aviary, Cindy. Show him the king parrots, they are moulting and if they are male, they will turn red from green. We won't know for a few months.' I said with a wink to Cindy.

'I would love to.' Joe's face lit up.

He stood and reached his hand out for Cindy and they walked off hand in hand.

'Kapai, I saw what you did there,' Tamati said, walking past me, but not touching me.

I grinned at him.

Maybe beer stopped him from wanting me. No more beer for him then. From crowd-hopping, I could safely say these guys were going to be my new friends. They all brought things to my life that I needed and would help me get over feeling sad about leaving my old friends in the city. Especially Jess. I felt like I could tell her anything and trust she would support me or pull me back in line. I was looking forward to starting school with them the following term, if everything went according to plan. Around eleven, the parents started gathering their teens.

Joe tried to hold Cindy but she shook him off. But then she said something in a whisper to him and he replied with, 'I can handle that, friends for now.' Joe would be back here in the morning with the cows. I bet she would be watching.

Sofie and Dave had been kissing a lot. Dave could hardly keep his hands off her. With all the visitors gone now, my cousins, Tamati, Basil and I moved inside to Tamati's new lounge room. We were singing songs and telling jokes while he played his guitar. I found an old harmonica of Uncle Jerry's, but none of us knew how to play, which made it even more fun. The twins went off to bed, followed closely by Cindy, and soon I was yawning too. My mission was to go to bed without a goodnight kiss, as Tamati kept saying we were just friends. Sadly, we'd acted like just friends for the last few hours. However, I'd noticed him watching me a lot.

I got up, 'Well, I better go.'

Tamati instinctively got up and our bodies connected at the entrance of the door. 'Should I walk you down to your room?' he asked.

I smiled instead of replying, and he walked down the hall. Our bodies which smelt of the good kind of smoke – bonfire smoke, kept touching, but we were not holding each other. As we got closer, we could hear some adults still outside. They had found some of Uncle Jerry's old whiskey. Sounded like they

were having a great time. We reached my
room, with still no contact but close enough
that there may as well have been.

I said, 'Good night Tamati,' and turned
around, but he just followed me into my
room and shut the door.

'I thought you were just walking me to my
room,' I said. 'After all, we are just friends.'
He looked hurt. So, I winked to reduce the
tension.

'You know, I think you're absolutely
amazing,' he said. 'Every day you surprise
me more. I feel like I've known you my
whole life and I want to see you every day
for the rest of my life. I'm gonna be fine
looking after this place when you go back
down to Auckland this week, but I don't
think I'm gonna be fine without you here.'

I didn't know what to say to him. He
was pouring his heart out to me. Or was
it the beer talking? I was so confused, so
obsessed with him, but I had to sort out
the Brandon thing. It would've been nice
to have been single for a little bit too. It
had been such a long time since I'd been
single. But this guy standing in front of
me, completely crazy for me, was the full

package. Everything I wanted in a guy. Kind heart, animal lover, quirky yet sensible. The fact that he was drop-dead gorgeous, and the most incredible kisser, was just a bonus.

'If you don't leave now, I'm going to attack you,' I said. 'That's not good, considering you are just my friend, so I'm going to say good night. I'll see you in the morning.'

He said, 'Good night,' closing the door on his way out.

Chapter 21: Markets
Belinda

Sometime during the night Tamati must have popped in to see me, as when I woke there was a flower beside my head, on my pillow. I put the flower in a glass of water on my desk, smiling. Tamati said he would sort the animals this morning and come to the markets later. We took three cars, packed with produce for the market. The twins in one, Charlie and Aunty in one, and Cindy, Mum, and I in the other. We set up and I was sweating before the crowd arrived. The day just got hotter and hotter and we got busier and busier. We needed all hands on deck. Mum and I quickly realised that if the others had not come to help for the market weekend, we wouldn't have been able to cope alone. It was too busy. Tamati, Jessica, and Wiremu came and helped so the rest of us could have a break and walk around. The minute Dave arrived, we lost Sofie.

Lily walked off with Elsa on her shoulders and Connor's arm around her. Connor and the twins were not the most helpful. Aunty was keen to bring her paintings to sell next time and was very inspired by the community. She took many photos of the markets and walked around the town taking photos of landscapes she would use as inspiration for paintings. She had fallen in love with this small town, and started talking about how they should move here, too. Especially seeing it looked like all their girls now had boyfriends up here. Well, no contact for Cindy, but in my eyes she was all loved up too. But I understood why Cindy needed time.

We made good money and split it with the others. Mum and I didn't want any, as we had enough. Tamati and Wiremu walked off for a while, leaving Jessica with me.

Jessica said, 'Are you sure nothing is going on with you and Tamati? You would be perfect together.'

'I know,' I said without thinking.

Oops, I covered my mouth, and she laughed.

A few people were selling second-hand bikes, and I bought them all. The five of us girls all rode a bike back home. It took us an hour with all the scenery stops, but we had nothing else we needed to do for the day. Having money was wonderful, but the fun with the girls was better. As we biked along, we were singing, talking about boys, and laughing as we pedaled our way to my place. It was just as rich an experience as any shopping spree would ever be, until my bike chain fell off, and we all pulled over. None of us knew what to do, so we started pushing the bikes.

'So, Bee, are you going to tell us what's really going on with Tamati?' Jess asked as we walked along the country road.

'He likes you!' Lily laughed.

'She likes him,' Sofie added.

'I caught them kissing,' Cindy said.

'Cindy!' I scolded.

The others all giggled, 'What?'

I then told them all about the dilemma I had with Brandon and Tamati. Sadly, Cindy showed them Brandon's Instagram, which was full of photos of him and I.

'Oh my gosh, you look like prom king and queen.' Jess said.

'They were,' Cindy laughed.

'Don't remind me.' I rolled my eyes. I'd hated that night. Brandon was so focused on being perfect we had no fun.

Cindy accidentally liked one photo.

'Cindy, unlike it now!' I yelled. She did, but not quick enough.

Brandon messaged her, '*Cindy, do you know where Bee is?*'

'Shit, what shall I do?' Cindy asked.

'Ignore it.' I said.

'You can't. He can see that she has read the message,' Lily said.

'This is why I don't do social media. It causes drama,' I replied.

'Tell him we have lost our Uncle and she will be home soon,' Lily said.

'Say that she was closer to Uncle Jerry than we realised, and she has a lot to sort out,' Sofie added.

'Say that she's in love. You don't have to say it's not with him.' Jess laughed.

'Shut up.'

Thankfully, a young guy came along and asked if we needed help. Even if he couldn't help with the chain at lease the subject had changed.

'Bee needs help with her love life,' Jess laughed.

'Who's Bee?' he asked, grinning a lopsided smile.

The girls all pointed at me.

'I can see why. You are beautiful. Can I take you out, Bee?' he asked.

'Sorry, I have farm work to do.'

He helped me fix my bike and left me his phone number before driving off. The girls were laughing so much as I ripped up the sleeze's phone number that Cindy dropped her bike.

Late afternoon after Jess had gone out with Wiremu, our family had an early roast lamb dinner before the cousins headed back to the city. Tamati was collecting his dragon from his uncle's place. Mum was reading a book on how to manage a farm, from the amazing library upstairs, and I found it all too quiet. Alone, I took Basil for a walk. We wandered in a paddock I hadn't seen before. Basil was digging away in a pile of dirt, barking. Suddenly his bark changed from excited to alarming. He started spinning in circles and jumping up and down, barking louder. Rushing closer, I saw something that looked out of place. I pulled it out slowly and saw blood. Blood? Why would a bloody cloth be buried in a plastic ziplock bag. I scrambled for my phone and actually had it for once, so I called the police. 'This is Belinda Loveridge.'

'Hi Bee,' Sargent Smith said.

'Basil and I were walking.' I paused, not sure how to say it. What if it was nothing?

'What did you find?'

Inside was a collection of items. I wasn't sure what, but I could make out a few things. 'Blood and pills, I think.'

'Stay put, we will find you.'

It took fifteen minutes till I heard the sirens and another ten for them to find us. More dramas.

'Here! We're over here!' I called out as Basil barked.

'Bee – are you okay?' Mum ran behind the police, panic etched on her face.

Tamati's normally sun-kissed skin was as white as mine. 'What happened?'

I pointed, no words; my body was shaking with the chills, and it had nothing to do with the weather. The police investigator searched in coveralls and gloves while Mum held me.

'Why didn't you call us?' Tamati asked.

'I called the police out of instinct, sorry.' I wasn't sure why I hadn't called them. The police numbers grew and grew. Lines of them walking and searching and again, we were asked to stay out of the way. Tamati, Basil and I went to the stables and spent the next hour rearranging the store cupboard with the odd distraction of mane brushing. Finally, the police left and Mum called Tamati and me over for a snack of left-over roast chicken.

'Do I have one less chicken?' I asked Mum.

'You have a few less. Home kill came over and we filled up the freezer.'

'But the freezer was full.'

'The police took the frozen meat.'

'Why?'

'I found some pills inside a chicken I was preparing for dinner the other day but didn't want to tell you.'

'Why?' seemed to be the only word I could say.

'You have enough on your shoulders with the animals – let me take some of the burden.'

'You are helping Mum – the money. Sorry, I didn't tell you.'

Tamati and Mum did the dishes while I took Marmalade out of her hidden spot and had a long shower with her. I put her in my room with Honey for the night and turned on an audio book. I was dreading tomorrow, but somehow, fell asleep. Monday was horrible. We had to pack up and head back to our home in Auckland.

'Tamati, promise you will look after the animals for me?' I begged as I was sitting on his lap on a pile of hay in the stables. He was running his hand over my hair and kissing my face.

'Promise you will break up with that guy?' he asked me.

'I promise,' I said, kissing him back.

He lay on top of me, and I could feel his body wanting me, needing me. We were about to take another step closer to each other when I heard Mum's car pull up and beep. Tamati breathed out, 'Ohhhhh you are going to be the death of me,'

Grinning at him, I winked.

'I'm going to miss you,' he said, giving me one last sweet kiss.

'I'm going to be yours,' I said, running off and jumping in the car.

As we drove through town, Mum got a call to pop into the police station. We stopped. Our lawyer was there working on something else. Small town, I thought. It felt like I was a criminal being led into a sterile interview room. Our lawyer joined us with several plain clothes police, including Sargent Smith.

'I am sorry to tell you this, but Jerry was murdered. It looked like natural causes, as you know, but we did still have our suspicions. His autopsy showed nothing. However, the package Belinda found yesterday had both Nigel and Jerry's blood on it.'

'Nigel's?' I asked.

'Looks like Jerry fought his killers and, although there was no evidence on him, the blood tells a different story.'

'Did he suffer?' Mum asked.

'Sorry,' a lady officer said. What kind of answer was that? I felt sick, I had hoped they hadn't hurt him? Poor Uncle Jerry. Three are caught, and Murray better not be tormenting him on the other side.

'One of the three caved in and told us everything last night. We have moved him to a different prison, and we will start a murder trial in due course.' I wanted to ask if it was Nigel – I still wanted to believe deep inside he was good but I didn't want to interrupt.

'Thank you for telling us. Do you need anything else?' Mum trembled.

'Access to the property.'

'We are away this week – Tamati, our farm hand is there.'

'I know Tamati,' the same female said. I looked at her, feeling green. How did she know him?

'Yes, you arrange access with your cousin,' a man said to her. I felt relieved that Tamati would sort this for us.

'We will complete a thorough search of the property using human resources and technology.'

'That's fine – thank you' I squeaked. Mum nodded. We walked to the car. I was in shock and didn't want to talk, so I listened quietly. First, as Mum called Tamati to update him and left him instructions, then Charlie when she told him the facts. Finally, Mum talked to her sister until we lost reception. That chat was all about emotions — emotions I was trying to push down inside my belly. I didn't even want to tell Mum how I was feeling. I didn't want to talk at all, so the second she hung up the phone, I turned Queen on the radio and sung at the top of my lungs to drown out my thoughts. Murder. One of four of the men I had constantly been alone with was not only capable of murder but *had* murdered. They'd killed my uncle and may have been planning to kill me next. I sang the next line – sang to forget.

Chapter 22: The City

Belinda

On Tuesday, I woke up in the city, traffic noise instead of animals. 'I hate it here,' I said to Mum. 'I want to go home. This place isn't home anymore.' Although the farm had memories of those horrible men it also had the animals. I was used to being there. This place had memories of just one horrible man, and that man could show up at any time. I needed to get away from my father before he found out about the farm and ruined that like he'd ruined everything else in my life.

'I agree,' she said. 'You need to go to school, do your speech and round off the term. You need credits to get into vet school. We will head back to the Manor on Friday night. Say your goodbyes. I'll resign today and organise the removal people to take our furniture to the Manor. Then we'll be able to rent this place out. However you will have to come stay with Daisy and sit your NCEA exams here. Starting a new school next year.

'I can handle that, thanks Mum,' I said, kissing her cheek, before putting my green and gold school uniform on for the fourth to last time. Even though the police were there, and uncle had been murdered there, I wanted to go back to the Manor. This world felt like a fake world now. My real world was with Tamati and the animals.

At school I said little, I studied hard. My best friend, Daisy, wanted to talk, but I kept her at arm's length. I would tell her everything, but my head was still spinning. I didn't even know what to say, *hey I own a farm, a business, illegal frogs, oh, and I cheated on Brandon—kinda*. Best to say nothing.

It was lunchtime before I saw Brandon. 'Hi,' I said, once I knew I couldn't avoid him.

'Hey,' he ran to hug me, 'I have missed you.'

'Really?' I asked, surprised.

'Did you not see my messages?'

'No.'

'Have you not been on Instagram?' he said.

'No, you know I don't like social media.' I exhaled in frustration. This was what our last fight had been about.

'I have no money on my phone to text,' he told me.

'I was sad you didn't message me at all,' I admitted, 'But I have hardly seen you for months, so I thought you were ghosting me, your way of ending things.'

'No way,' he said, leaning in for a kiss.

I lifted my hand up in front of my face, stopping the incoming kiss.

'Brandon, I am ending things between us.'

'What?' he said in alarm.

'Friday is my last day of school. We are moving out of town.'

'Why?' he asked. I could see tears forming in his eyes. Maybe he did like me. Had he just forgotten to put the effort in?

'Because it's time for a change,' I said honestly. I used to think he was the most attractive guy; I didn't see any of that now. When I closed my eyes, all I saw was Tamati. Tamati on a horse, Tamati feeding a lizard, Tamati chasing a bird. I had to refocus on the scene at hand. The scene Tamati would like.

'But what about us?'

'There hasn't been an us for ages. I never see you.'

'Yes, there has, look on Instagram,' he said.

'No, I live in the real-world Brandon. The last few times we have hung out, we have been in groups, or you have played on your phone, or we just made out. No talking, laughing, connecting, or having fun together. That's not being in a relationship. Sorry, we are over. I have to go. Thanks for the good times,' I said, walking off.

An enormous burden had been lifted. I sat at a bench seat alone and messaged Jess, Cindy, and Tamati and said, *I'm officially single.*' All three of them messaged me something along the lines of *Not for long.*

Mum also sent me a text *You have been accepted at the school up north next year.*

After school I wandered home, talking to Tamati on the Air Pods as I went. I walked down the long driveway to our house. Mum had been busy. There was already a 'for rent' sign up outside. There was a bunch of flowers at the back door, so I picked it up and put the flowers in a vase inside. All our vases were already full of tokens of sympathy. It was only then that I read the note. It was from Brandon. I was still processing that when there was a knock on the door. 'Oh, hey Brandon.'

'Please Bee, you and I are soul mates. We can do the long-distance thing; I have my license now and Dad got me a car to share with my sister.'

How awkward. Tamati was still on the phone and could hear everything Brandon said.

'Is that your ex?' Tamati asked in my Air Pods.

'Sorry Brandon. Like I said earlier, you and I have been over for a while. As you can see by looking around, we are leaving town. Our relationship's finished.'

He was crying.

'If that was me, I would want a hug. Sounds like you broke him.' Tamati said in my ear.

I opened my arms, and Brandon walked into them.

'Sorry that you didn't want us to be over. I wish you all the best. I really do.'

'One last kiss?' Brandon said, as he pressed his lips on mine.

'No!' Tamati whispered in my ear.

'No, and when did you start smoking? Gross! Please have better respect for your body. 'Thankfully, Mum arrived home and I said, 'Brandon was just leaving.' I couldn't escape the smell of smoke.

Brandon finally left and with a bag full of clothes and a hockey ball he had stored at my place.

When he'd left Mum said, 'I was going to ask him to stay for dinner. I have made too much.'

Tamati laughed in my ear. 'She always does.'

'We've broken up, Mum. I was struggling to get rid of him, thanks.' I stormed off to my room.

'Never a dull moment with you,' Tamati laughed in my ear.

'At least you know what you are in for,' I laughed, hoping he wouldn't run for the hills.

'Where do I sign up?' he joined me laughing.

'Don't you have work to do?' I asked him. 'How are all my babies?'

'Every single one of them is missing you. They are not coping and need you back here.'

'Do they now? Or do you?' I asked.

'All of us,' he said. 'Oh bugger. Sorry, gotta go, just got a call out. See you soon and stay away from Brandon. By the way, I hate smoking too.'

'Good. Catch ya.'

Wednesday at school, I headed straight to Daisy. She was talking to a guy and looked frustrated at me, but I didn't care.

'Daisy, yesterday I broke up with Brandon.'

'What?' she interrupted me.

'Shh,' I hushed her. She pretended to lock her lips as I told her everything. She stuck beside me in the rest of our classes now that she knew I was leaving at the end of the week. She promised to come and stay with me in the holidays and not to tell anyone else where I was. She couldn't wait for me to stay with her at exam time and for senior prize-giving. She understood that no one could know in case Dad ever came around asking. She had a useless father and understood about my Dad more than anyone else did.

Mum and I were packing the last of our stuff on Thursday night when there was a knock on the front door. I thought it was the pizza getting delivered and opened it without paying attention.

Big mistake! Shocked, I let the familiar man push past me and I closed the door behind him.

'Mum!' I called, without being able to hide the panic in my voice.

'What's up?' Mum said, emptying the last of the pot cupboard.

'Oh!' she said when she saw him.

He was the love of her life, and the reason she was happily single.

'What's going on here?' Dad asked, brushing his hand over a bunch of flowers with anger.

'We are moving to Timbuktu,' I said, matching his anger levels.

'Watch that mouth of yours. You're not too old for a spanking, child!'

I rolled my eyes. Some things never changed. Last time he'd showed up we hadn't seen him in three years. He'd come back and Mum had thought it would finally work out for them. He'd only stayed for four months. Mum had gone out to the supermarket and came back to find him gone, having taken whatever he could find of value with him, including the money that Mum had been saving for my school camp. Aunty Carol had paid for my camp fees in the end. At the time, I didn't understand why she'd had to take Mum away for a week. Mum was so depressed. I wanted to help her, but I'd stayed with Daisy. I never questioned Mum about that time, but she came back with marks on her wrists that I could still see some days. This fueled my anger for Dad even more. I would not lose my mum because of my manipulative father.

I thought he had gone from our lives but he stood in the lounge, amongst the packed boxes and blooming flowers, frowning at me. I glared at him with my hands on my hips. 'What do you want, Dad?'

His body language changed from aggressive to welcoming.

'Just kidding, come hug your old man,' he said. 'I bought you a gift.'

'My birthday was three months ago,' I told him. 'Not a card or anything, then!'

He reached into his pocket and brought out a slightly warm chocolate bar.

'Thanks,' I said.

'What do you want, Shane?' Mum asked, too.

'You,' Dad said, walking over to Mum and reaching out to hold her, as he did. 'I watched a romantic movie last night, and I realised what I was missing. I'm so sorry for all the bad times, Tasha. From now on, it's only good times. He started kissing her neck, and her body gave in.'

'Here we go again,' I said under my breath. Why couldn't we have left one day earlier? How long till Dad left her again this time? Why did she always take him back?

Mum finally pulled away. 'It's good you are here. Please sign our divorce papers.'

Mum handed him some forms. Dad just ripped the papers up. He picked mum up and carried her to the bedroom. Mum was the strongest person I knew, unless Dad was involved. After packing up the kitchen, I went to my room to put my headphones in. I sent a text to Aunty, telling her that Dad was with Mum, before I dropped my phone and curled into a ball. We should never have come back here.

Tamati called me. His voice was high pitched, with eagerness. 'Hey, we've got an egg cracking. I wonder what kind of bird it will be,' he said.

I took a big breath, but a sob escaped.

'What's wrong?'

I told him everything. Then I went to sleep listening to him playing the guitar over the phone.

Dad dropped me off at school the next morning. He said he would pick me up after school. Bloody father of the year.

I was pleasantly surprised when Mum collected me from school at lunchtime.

'What about Dad?' I asked.

'He thinks we are moving south,' she said. 'Sorry about last night.'

'Are you okay?' I asked.

'Closure, but no divorce.'

'Sorry, Mum.'

'It's okay. He gave me you, the best thing that has ever happened to me.'

We popped home one last time and cleared out all our stuff.

With goldfish in a bag on my lap, cats and rabbits in cages in the back, the music pumped up and the two of us singing out of tune, Mum backed out of the driveway.

It started to rain, as my childhood house faded into the distance. I thought about the seed pods on the ground with their strong stink. The good and bad memories would linger. But fresh adventures lay ahead.

Chapter 23: Shot

Tamati had headed off to the city for Uni – I couldn't believe how I was relying on him not just with the animals. My babies – my responsibility. I got up, I would say early but that's the only time of the day to get up - when the birds get up. I listened to the moreporks final call of the morning, as I headed over to the shed. I love that the moreporks are free as they should be.

Stopped in my tracks by the smell. I wasn't dreaming it. It wasn't stale, it was fresh – cigarette smell. I texted Mum and slowly opened the lizard shed. With my phone on silent, I took a photo and sent it to mum and to Sargent Smith before I put the phone back in my pocket. A very much alive Murray turned and saw me, his gun was pointed at my head before I could react.

'You little bitch – you have ruined everything.'

'You can have whatever you want.' I tried to sound strong but the quiver in my voice was giving me away. A gun was pointed at me by the man who had killed my Uncle Jerry.

'I will get revenge for the men who you put away.'

'B.. b.. but you were in the wrong... you kil...' I vomited all over the shed's concrete floor.

'Gross!' he screamed, taking a step back. And using an old towel to wipe my last night's dinner off his gumboots. I took that as my chance, and I opened the shed door and ran. My decision to run away from the house was the decision that saved my life. As I ducked behind an apple tree, Murray fired the gun five times in the other direction. Towards the house where my mum was. The noise was deafening –

if my text hadn't woken mum, she would be awake now. He stopped to reload as the sound of a window shattering echoed in the hills. I ducked down from the tree and lay flat in the scrub in case he turned around, which he did. As the deafening noise of firing bullets reached my ears, I heard a new sound. My heart was beating loudly in my chest, but the new sound was of sirens. The police were here. I would be saved.

I heard more bullets being loaded. Now what was he going to do – why wouldn't he give up. He waited till the police were out of their cars – bulletproof vests on and guns aimed at him, not knowing they were also aimed at me. Murray opened fire and just as the police retaliated, he ducked inside the shed. The police bullets shot my way, I rolled on my back and lifted my hands over my head. Pain, my eyes stung from crying, my ears rung from the sound, and my elbow was on fire as my arm collapsed to the hard cold ground. I screamed as police ran to the door and saw me.

'Is there another door out of this shed?' an officer yelled at me. Not are you okay?

'No,' I puffed in agony.

The police circled the shed, guns pointing and finally two of them supported me as I hobbled to the back of a police car, where Mum joined me. Leaving Murray surrounded by guns in our dust. We drove away and every bump in the drive causing shooting pain up my left arm. Even as we drove on the smoother country road, the pain didn't cease.

I was back in the local hospital, still in a moon boot, but now with my arm in a sling. This time there was no waiting around like my leg injury. They dashed me in a wheelchair off to a ward, where a huddle of doctors rushed in to see me. The ward was filled with police officers – as patients. All dripping with blood caused by Murray, caused by me. Before I could see what injuries I had, they moved me into a private room. The pain was intense as a nurse hunted for a vein. On his third attempt on my hand; he found one and the pain relief was dripped into my veins after the saline.

'Where is he?' I screamed as an officer walked past my room, looking at the door. The officer shook his head at me. Mum messaged Sargent Smith but got no reply.

There was a commotion, and the doctors all ran to a room down the hall. A nurse pulled mum back into the room as she tried to spy on the action.

'Please, is that drama because of my farm?' I sobbed. They had given me as much pain relief as they could, but it didn't help at all. I could still hear the gunshots, see the flashing lights when I closed my eyes. A police officer finally walked in to see me. The pain killers were not working but my head felt loose, almost not connected to my body. I tried to wriggle my toes and I didn't know if they moved or not. I wanted to ask what happened. But couldn't get the words out. Thankfully, Mum asked. My still body listened to the updates, and my eyes closed as they sobbed the tears that I thought had all dried up.

'Where is Sargent Smith?' mum's first question was asking after the man we wanted to ask the real question to – where was Murray?

The officer didn't answer. He shook his head and his formal posture shrunk.

'No,' I croaked, but no sound escaped.

'Sorry, there were some casualties,' the officer's feet twisted on the lino with a slight squeak.

'Was Sergeant Smith one of them?' Mum asked. The officer nodded. I know they're trying to stay professional but losing one of their own was too hard for this young officer. She wasn't crying yet, but mum and I both were allowed to, and I bet she would be the minute her shift ended. Mum asked the Murray question next. Shake of a head. 'He didn't make it.'

'Two casualties.' Mum said, her hand on her heart. 'Please tell me they were the only two casualties?'

Yes, so far, there are more injured, but nobody else appears critical.

The doctors arrive before the police officer could tell us anything else.

'Belinda needs an operation. We are sedating her now and just need your approval. I thought I would never close my eyes again because of the flashing lights, and the crashing, pinging, ringing in my ears, and I would never hear laughter again, but somehow, I fell asleep. Somehow, my mind drifted off to feathers, Tamati and I laughing on a bench surrounded by birds, Marmalade and Honey on each of my shoulders, and Basil at my feet, Paprika asleep on my chest. Both of my hands still functioned in the dream. My smile still shone, my life was happy, but those things were just dreams now.

Chapter 23: My Belinda

Tamati

If you had told me a few weeks ago that one person could completely change another person as much as Belinda had changed me, I would not have believed it.

I had a plan for life: work hard, play hard, screw harder.

This was the longest I had gone without sex for ages, also it was the most satisfied I had ever been.

Tash had given me free range on driving their cars, so I jumped in a Ferrari, 250 GTO yesterday. I'd driven north to see my iwi on the marae, and I was currently driving down to a university class.

I put a podcast on for the first part of the trip. I wanted to call my best mate Aidan, but it was too early, even for her.

Belinda thought I was an expert on dragons and lizards. I wasn't yet, but I wanted to be. So that was what all my podcasts had been about lately, and I'd already learnt so much. Belinda hung off every word I said about them, so at least I sounded like I knew my stuff.

At eight o'clock, it was late enough to call Aidan. 'Aidaaaaaan,' I sang when she answered the phone.

'Where are you?' She asked me, sounding panicked.

Belinda knew my best mate was Aidan. She just didn't realise that Aidan was a girl who I suspected may have feelings for me. I had made sure no one could see Aidan's face when I'd been on face chats.

'On my way,' I said.

'How far on your way? As in at the dairy and you're almost here or what?'

'I'm two hours away.' I said.

'Fuck,' she cursed.

'Sorry.'

'You're on speaker. Let's swat.'

'What's going on with you?'

'Later,' I promised. 'Please quiz me.'

Aidan, loyal as always, quizzed me for half an hour before ending the call. Then twenty minutes later she called me back and, on speaker, I listened to the beginning of the first lecture of the day.

I pulled up outside class and ran to the door.

'I'm outside,' I messaged Aidan.

I waited for her reply. 'Now.'

I slid quietly in the door and sat beside Aidan. She had already set out paper and pens and even made some notes for me.

'Nice of you to join us, Tamati,' Mr Penworth said. 'I will still have to mark you as absent.'

'I'm sorry, but I swear I've heard every word you said in class today.' I summarised his lesson so far and I saw him mark me as present.

I was studying on a scholarship and needed to make my classes. I had a grotty room in a shady flat close to uni but headed north when I could, I preferred the country to the city any day!

We were set an exercise and as we did it, the tutor came to see me.

'You missed class last Thursday and were late today?'

'Sorry, I listened to last week's classes. Here is my work.' I handed over a comprehensive assignment.

He smiled, flicking through it.

'I had food poisoning. I promise you, you did not want me here last week, Sir.'

'I have high expectations from you, Tamati, which means if you let me down, you have a bigger fall than others.'

'Yes Sir,' I said. 'Sorry. I swear I am focused.'

When class ended, I had thirty minutes till the next one. I kissed Aidan on the forehead and rushed out of class. I found Mandy easily enough. She was waiting for me outside the toilets. She grabbed my hand and pulled me into the disabilities cubical.

'Mandy, babe, sorry. We won't be doing this anymore,' I started.

'Why not?' she asked, putting her undies in my hand and bending over with her skirt flipped over her upper body.

'Thanks for the good times. Find yourself a good man, one who wants to wake up with you.' And I handed back her undies and walked out.

I strolled into the library, heading straight to the animal area and grabbed a few new books.

'Hey handsome,' Jaynee said. 'You stood me up last week.'

'Oh sorry, I was sick.' More like lovesick.

'Tonight?' she asked.

'I can't sorry, I'm off the market.'

'As in tied down?' she asked me.

'Very much so.'

'Who? Aidan? Lara?'

'No, her name is Belinda, and she's my everything.'

'Okay then,' she said. 'All good, 'cause I've had other offers.'

'I bet you have.' I squeezed her hand before I walked away. Then I heard her sniff. In the reflection, I saw her supervisor support her as she cried. Crap, what had I done? I did like Jaynee, but was never going to commit to her, or any of the others. I ran to the campus cafe and had a similar conversation there with Evie. Evie handed me the two coffees that I'd ordered and I ran back to the next class, giving one coffee to Aidan and I said, 'Thanks.'

'What's this for?' she asked.

'Being you. Thanks for covering for me and helping me study. I just realised that I have been a bit of a slut around here.'

'You can say that again.'

'Not anymore.'

'Really?' she asked as she leaned towards me. 'Oops.'

'I have a Belinda.' I said.

'You have a Belinda?' she questioned.

'That's why I was away last week. Belinda needed me.'

'Owww, has Belinda stolen your heart?' she asked.

I opened my phone and showed Aidan some photos of Belinda. Including some of her asleep.

'Are you a stalker? Does she know you photograph her while she sleeps?'

'No.' I laughed. I showed Aidan some photos of the animals.

'Was it her house you have been calling me from?'

'Yip,' I said.

'Wow. You have given up your wild and free lifestyle because some chick opens her legs for you.'

'Actually, she's a virgin.'

'Give me strength,' Aidan laughed. 'What happens when she puts out?'

'I'll put a ring on her finger.'

'Dude! how old is she?'

'Don't ask,' I puffed my checks out and looked at the ceiling. We had our next class and as the teacher took the roll, my phone vibrated. It was Tasha. I ignored it but texted *is everything okay?* She called again.

'Sorry Sir, – I have to take this.'

'Sit down,' I heard the teacher say as I closed the door behind me.

'Hi,' I answered.

'When are you back? Can you look after the animals?'

'When, for how long? Where's Bee?' I stumbled on my words. Where is Bee? I wanted to scream, why was she calling me instead of Bee? The phone was silent for far too long – well, not silent. I could hear deep breathing. What was she not saying?

'Tasha, what's happened?'

'Murray,' she finally hissed.

'He's dead.' I knew he was dead – an exploding truck a few days earlier.

'Yes, he is. But he was at the farm this morning,'

'What? But he's dead now?'

'Yes.'

'Where's Bee?' I asked again, sliding down the wall on the cold corridor and hugging my knees to my chest.

'She was shot.'

'What? Shot. By Murray?' My body shaking.

'No, shot by the police – she's, she, well she can't manage the animals and there are bullet holes in the house and aviary. We may have lost animals and birds. I really don't know. But Bee was shot.' Tasha almost sounded like a stranger, her voice was deeper, and she spoke with gaps between every word, and a sob escaped as she stopped speaking.

'I am on my way.' I hung up. I was not going for the animals. I wanted to be there when Bee woke up. I charged into class and said, 'sorry Sir, I have to go.'

He said 'sit down...' until he saw my face red and wet with pain.

'My girlfriend's been shot.' I pushed out the last of my breath before throwing my books in my bag and leaving.

I didn't listen to music or podcasts or anything. All I did was count the corners in the road until I could see Bee. My rushing was all in vain because when I arrived at the hospital, they wouldn't let me see her so I went to the farm and they wouldn't let me in there either. I had to go to my uncle's place.

'Uncle Mark, please help me.' I sobbed as I walked into the vet shed at the front of his farmlet.

'What's wrong?' he asked, stepping away from the computer and coming to my side.

I told him what I knew about the police and Murray shootout.

'I heard there was something happening with the police.'

'One of them shot Bee.' My tears increased.

'Bee is off limits to you.' He held out an arm.

I fell into his embrace, letting all my fears and emotions out. I'd never cried over a chick before, but Bee – she was different. 'We are not together.'

'But?' he asked, patting my back as the father figure he'd become.

'I love her.'

'I see that. The last thing that family needs is you breaking that little girl's heart.'

'I know.' I sobbed. Enough tears. I pulled my big boy pants up.

'Come on, let's go.'

I helped Uncle Mark fill the truck with wire and board and animal first aid bags. With my uncle beside me, we were given access to the property. First, we secured the wired fencing near the animals. Uncle also called the glass company to fix the broken windows. I'm actually glad Bee wasn't with us because we had to put a few lovely birds down, and some had escaped through bullet holes in the aviary. Mainly, the animal deaths were in the shed. I wanted to clean up the blood on the floor but could only tend to the animals, as we had a police chaperone.

Was any of the blood Bee's? If so, how much? I wanted to ask. Instead, I focused on what I could do. Make the place clean for when Bee returned, and she would not want to see her babies dead. Guinea pigs, water dragons, bearded dragons, mice. So many dead animals, so we bagged up the shot creatures and changed water and topped bowls up again, and fed the living ones. I even gave out treats. They deserved it.

The room reeked of iron and gunpowder, not a smell these animals were used to. Any that were injured we couldn't save but Uncle Mark dealt with them. I should have, but I was too on edge about knowing if Bee was okay to do that kind of horrible work today. We repaired enclosures (it took a few hours).

I saw a galah on the apple tree outside trying to get back in to its mate. I held out my hand, and he flew back to me. I walked around for a while, whistling and staying out of the investigator's way as much as possible. I managed to find a handful of other birds and place them back in cages. I checked on the pets in the house, and the horses, then begged Uncle Mark to go to the hospital with me.

The hospital still wouldn't let me see Bee. I called Tasha and her phone went to the answering machine. Outside a group of police walked past – their body language drooped as they spoke in hushed tones. I followed to hear what they were saying. 'I can't believe she died, too. Her shots didn't seem as bad.'

'Days like these make working this job hard.' Another officer said before they walked out of range.

'Surely they were talking about someone else,' Uncle Mark said. Id forgotten he was with me, but he was supporting my eavesdropping. I bet my face was as pale as fresh snow. Uncle Mark called his mate Jake Smith. He was the lead on the case. No reply – he called Dave Thomson next. Dave did answer, but he was crying and said he couldn't officially say anything, but it had been the worst day ever.

I stayed at my uncle's that night on his couch. No sleep. I didn't know if she was okay. Surely if she was okay, she would have called. No call meant trouble. The next morning, I still couldn't get hold of Tasha or Bee, so I borrowed my cousin's phone and looked on social media for Bee's cousins – no luck. Uncle and I went back to the farm and tended to the animals before I camped outside the hospital reading the news, waiting to be allowed in. Even the people in the waiting rooms moved slower than normal, talked slowly in blurry voices.

Had Belinda died? Would I feel it? I looked up at the local news. Three dead in police incident in Northland. Three. Murray, and who? Belinda. I couldn't handle it anymore.

I paced the waiting room, and when a couple were led down the corridor for an appointment, I followed. An orderly swiped their card and the three of us walked through. As they turned left to the cardio ward. I headed off, looking in all the rooms. So many rooms, but finally, I found her. Tasha and Bee were sleeping. I snuck in and gave her a kiss on her warm cheek. Warm – she was alive. She was shot, but alive. Her right arm was connected to a drip and her left arm was bandaged, but I could still see blood.

Her beautiful eyes fluttered open, and I pulled my hand to her lips, begging her to stay quiet so I could connect with her before her mum woke.

She was the most beautiful girl I'd ever seen – even in the hospital. My relief that she was alive pulsed through me.

Her lips parted enough to share a smile, then my lips were on hers. Our lips danced together until she groaned with delight, so I stepped away. Good thing too, as Tasha woke up.

'Tamati?'

'Hi, sorry to wake you. I couldn't get hold of you and wanted to see if you were both okay.

'It hurts.' she said.

'Where?'

With a grunt, she brought her hands to her heart. She must have really seen some horrible things. I tell her about the animals and birds I saved and what I'd repaired. Then a team of doctors came and kicked me out. I went home and called Aidan, and we spent the rest of the day studying and doing homework while I bonded with Bee's pets.

Chapter 24: Sunshine
Tamati

Tamati

A month later and life was back to normal. My exams and study were over for the year, Bee had ended up sitting her exams with the help of the northern health school and together we were looking after the animals. It was a more manageable number of animals and didn't consume our days, but we took our time doing it.

We lay enjoying the sunshine. Bee really wanted to go horse riding and bike riding and kayaking, doing whatever the youth group was doing this weekend. But no - she had to stay put, which was not her strength – but we studied a lot. I started reading vet books to her and we would lay in the stables or aviary or even sheep paddocks for hours and I would read. She would question everything. There was still so much that she didn't know about me. So much. We couldn't be together yet, but we would bide our time. Our future would be something worth dreaming about.

The End.

Acknowledgements

Tonchi, Marco, Lucas, and Frankie you are my everything.

Special thanks to Val, Diana and Glen, thanks for your constant support.

Anna McKersey - I wouldn't have shared any of my writing without your encouragement.

Vicki Arnott and Melissa Guyon for your fabulous editing and teaching me along the way.

Ashley Lindsay for helping me finesse and enrich my ideas.

The members of the Auckland Writer's group and Scriptorium for all your wisdom, friendship, and inspiration.

Sue Russell – thanks for being my constant cheerleader and helping me overcome critique without collapsing in a corner.

The Bird Barn specifically Sydney for your advice and poses. Wade Hason for your Law advice. DOC, Auckland Zoo, Unitec and Auckland Museum for your insights.

To the Auckland writers, RWNZ (Romance Writers of New Zealand), NZSA (New Zealand Society of Authors) and Storyline for all you have taught me at conferences and workshops and the friends and support I have met along the way.

To all the Arts of Development Performers. Thanks for your stories and helping me keep my pulse on the thoughts of today's youth.

To my beta readers Lucas, Asha, Holly and Jazmine

Other Titles by Sue Carpenter

The Summer Job

Sandra is determined to prove herself as she tries out for a summer lifesaving job – a job that will take her away from the safety of the farm into the unknown. But Sandra isn't expecting to meet someone who will change her life. She soon discovers that people can be manipulative and deceitful. Will she navigate the turbulent waters of first love and a new job.

The Dramatic Bubble

Kenzie wants to focus on her school exams with no distractions, but cupid, COVID and the government have other ideas. Will the Catholic boy be a distraction for her, or the only thing that holds her together as her family life collapses?

Lavender and Pearls

Jackie and her brother Hayden are sent to stay at their eccentric Aunt's Antique shop in New Zealand, where they discover a magical secret. When her family members start to go missing, Jackie must venture into fantastical and dangerous new lands to save them. Will Jackie rescue her family? And what secrets will she discover along the way?

Sue Carpenter

Sue is a Junior Fiction and Young Adult Author.

She had learning issues growing up, but an active imagination. As an adult she doesn't want her readers to need a dictionary to fall into her imaginary worlds.

Sue is not ready to grow up yet and keeps her mind young by writing for children and spending time with her three sons.

To find more of Sue's work follow her on Instagram susieleenz

https://linktr.ee/susieleenz?fbclid=IwAR1
LZZJ-_yLghG1kZ9m9bXWh47vFqWXc5UiE6
OdOeEG9uvDhAWFjmJFslFQ

www.ingramcontent.com/pod-product-compliance
Lightning Source LLC
Chambersburg PA
CBHW061649190726

48289CB00006B/1801